"Solana has long been one of the quirkiest and most accomplished of crime writers, but this is something new — wonderfully crafted short-form fiction – often sardonic, often surreal, but always pure Solana."

BARRY FORSHAW, AUTHOR OF *EURO NOIR*

"Teresa Solana's distinctive writing is humorous yet thought-provoking, and her short fiction is as entertaining as her novels."

MARTIN EDWARDS, AUTHOR OF
GALLOWS COURT AND *THE LAKE DISTRICT MYSTERIES*

"Detective fiction in Spain is flourishing and Teresa Solana is one of its most accessible protagonists. Her books are superbly plotted, as well as being sharp and acerbically funny commentaries on a society still coming to terms with Franco's dictatorship. The present collection, brilliantly translated by Peter Bush, brings together her explorations of the darker side of contemporary Barcelona and her unsettling surrealistic streak."

PAUL PRESTON, AUTHOR OF *THE SPANISH CIVIL WAR*

"*The First Prehistoric Serial Killer* is a delight. Teresa Solana romps through a louche Barcelona teeming with shady characters and criminal intent. Whether investigating the titular crime, smoking out a grand house's generations of ghosts, or connecting the dots between a series of events, her signature combination of dark humour and sly social commentary informs every word. She's aided and abetted by her usual partner in crime, translator Peter Bush, who renders her tales in sparkling English."

SUSAN HARRIS, *WORDS WITHOUT BORDERS*

Born in Barcelona in 1962, Teresa Solana lives in Oxford. She has written several highly acclaimed novels. *A Not So Perfect Crime*, the first in the Borja and Eduard crime series, won the 2006 Brigada 21 Prize for the best Catalan crime novel. Since then, she has published five more novels. In addition to many articles and essays on translation, Teresa Solana has also written a number of children's books.

Peter Bush is an acclaimed translator from Spanish and Catalan, known for his translations of Leonardo Padura, Juan Goytisolo and Josep Pla.

THE FIRST PREHISTORIC SERIAL KILLER

AND OTHER STORIES

Teresa Solana

Translated from the Catalan by Peter Bush

BITTER LEMON PRESS
LONDON

BITTER LEMON PRESS

First published in the United Kingdom in 2018 by
Bitter Lemon Press, 47 Wilmington Square, London WC1X 0ET

www.bitterlemonpress.com

The *Blood, Guts and Love* stories were first published in Catalan as part of
Set casos de sang i fetge i una història d'amor by Edicions 62, Barcelona, 2010.
The stories in *Connections* were first published in Catalan as *Matèria Grisa* by
Amsterdam, Ara Llibres, Barcelona, and received the Roc Boronat Prize 2017.

Versions of some of the stories in this collection have previously been published in
the *Ellery Queen Mystery Magazine, The Massachusetts Review* and *Mediterraneans*. 'The
Son-in-Law' appeared in both in the *Words Without Borders Best of the First Ten Years*
anthology and the *Found in Translation* anthology of the best hundred stories in
world literature from Head of Zeus. *Connections* won the prestigious Catalan 2107
Roc Boronat prize, and 'Still Life No. 41' was shortlisted for the 2013 Edgar award.

The translation of this work has been supported by the Institut Ramon Llull.

©Teresa Solana 2018
English translation ©Peter Bush 2018

A CIP record for this book is available from the British Library

ISBN 978–1–912242–07-8
eBook ISBN 978–1–912242–08-5

Typeset by Tetragon
Printed and bound in Great Britain by
Clays Ltd, St Ives plc

LLLL institut
ramon llull
Catalan Language and Culture

Contents

BLOOD, GUTS
AND LOVE

A first note to readers:

Can you imagine living in a house haunted by ghosts with class prejudice? Or being a prehistoric detective on the verge of becoming the first religious charlatan, investigating a triple murder that is threatening blissful cave life? Or running an art gallery where stinking statues decompose on their pedestals? These stories combine absurd humour with noir to paint a satirical portrait of the society in which we live.

Most readers and writers of noir will never commit a crime or be involved in a police investigation, and perhaps that is why we so enjoy reading and writing stories of blood and guts that allow us to enter the criminal minds of murderers and the elaborate mind games and procedures of fictional detectives. But we are all trapped in some way. No matter whether a tormented ghost, a repentant vampire, a nice-as-pie old lady or a gauche mammoth hunter, at some stage in our lives we will be forced to make a choice that will challenge our values and force us to enter the murky unknown.

The First Prehistoric Serial Killer

A number of us woke up this morning when the storm broke, only to find another corpse in the cave. This time it was Athelstan. I almost fainted the second I saw his smashed skull and his brains seeping down his temples into a pool of black blood, but the others slapped me and I came around. I rushed to rouse our chief to ask him to come and take a look and tell us what to do. Ethelred is on the deaf side and sleeps like a log, and though the men shouted, in the end we had to piss on him to get him to stir. Grumbling and bleary-eyed, our chief examined Athelstan's body, cursing our bones for dragging him out of bed at such an early hour. In the meantime, the rain stopped and the sun began to shine.

While Ethelred and the others speculated about what had happened, I studied the bloody rock that lay a few yards from Athelstan's corpse and suggested to Ethelred that the two might be related. Ethelred, a rather laconic troglodyte, looked at me sceptically and warned me not to jump to conclusions.

"Hold your horses," he commented. "I want my breakfast first."

After gobbling down fried ostrich eggs with turtle and herb sausages, Ethelred calmed his men down by insisting it must have been an accident. Then he brushed his teeth on a branch and said he'd like to speak to me in private. We surreptitiously retreated to a recess at the back of the cave so the other males wouldn't hear our conversation, but as our cave has magnificent acoustics and you have to shout at Ethelred to make sure he hears you, everybody eavesdropped. In fact, I didn't see the point of so much secrecy, because he soon called an assembly to inform the men, and, except for Rufus, who's rather nosy, nobody seemed particularly interested.

Ethelred, who isn't as stupid as he seems, asked me to open an investigation because three deaths in fourteen moons are too many and the clan was beginning to feel edgy. The fact that all three had been male and that we'd found them early in the morning with their heads smashed in with a rock was too much of a coincidence. However, cautious Rufus and Ethelred favour the accident hypothesis. For my part, I'm pretty sure something's up in the cave. My problem is I don't know what.

Rufus, Ethelred's right-hand man, immediately protested at the very idea that I should lead the investigation, but Ethelred quickly landed a punch, and knocked a couple of his teeth out: end of argument. It makes a lot of sense that he's chosen me to handle this; I am, by a long chalk, the cleverest troglodyte ever. Of the twenty males that comprise the Hairy Bear tribe (give or take a couple), I'm the only one who doesn't stumble over the same stone every morning when I leave the cave, a phenomenon that intrigues the lot of them. The other point in my favour is that I'm the troglodyte with most free time on his hands because Ethelred has banned me from going hunting. Partly because I'm not very good at it and he prefers me to stay with the females rather than upset the hunting party. Indeed, if I hadn't discovered fire by chance one spring evening when the other males were out shafting and I was bored stiff, they'd have probably put me six feet under and I'd be pushing up daisies in the necropolis or in some animal's craw. After all, thinking with one's head and not one's feet (or that other appendage …) has its advantage, and I trust that I'll get recognition someday.

Because of my privileged status as the idler in the tribe, I had no choice but to follow Ethelred's orders. He's in charge and, however much we grumble about it, this is no democracy. As the rain had stopped, the men went mammoth hunting and the women snail collecting; in the meantime, I slumped under a fig tree and activated my grey cells to find a lead to help me discover the murderer's identity. Ethelred and Rufus can say what they like, but I am convinced there's skulduggery afoot and we're dealing with three murders, with a capital M.

The first to cop it was Lackland, whose head was also smashed in with a bloody stone that was then left lying next to it. Lackland was a fine fellow but daft as a brush, so we all thought it was self-inflicted and left it at that. A few moons later it was Beowulf's turn, and since he mostly received blows to the right side of his skull, I started to think we were barking up the wrong tree. Everyone in the clan knew Beowulf was left-handed (because his right arm had ended up in some beast's belly), so it could hardly have been suicide or an accident, which had been our theory in Lackland's case. My suspicions were confirmed this morning when we found Athelstan's corpse. At a glance the cause of death seems similar, but as nobody knows how to carry out an autopsy *comme il faut*, we can't be sure. In the absence of scientific evidence, I must tread the slippery terrain of hypothesis where it's easy to come a cropper. Nonetheless, I think there are three facts I can establish beyond the shadow of a doubt: firstly, all three met a violent death; secondly, someone smashed their skulls in with a rock; thirdly, it happened while they were sleeping, because we found all three on the pile of rotting leaves we call a bed.

Far be it from me to seem melodramatic, but considering that the modus operandi seems to be the same in each case, I'm beginning to think we are dealing with the first prehistoric serial killer ever. The fellow who did it has bumped off three men and we've yet to find him, so I deduce he must be a cold, calculating male, and brainy into the bargain.

Mid-morning the hunters returned with a couple of mammoths. There were no casualties on this occasion. After clearing it with Ethelred, I started my interrogations and spoke to every member of the tribe to see if anyone was without an alibi. Unfortunately, they all had one, because they swore to a man they were snoozing in the cave. As I'd spent the night at the necropolis reflecting on the question of existence, I realized I was the only one without a rock-solid alibi. But I'd swear I didn't kill Athelstan. I'm almost absolutely sure on that front.

Given that everyone has an alibi, I concluded we were perhaps looking in the wrong place. Not far from our cave there's a small hamlet of stone houses we call Canterbury because the inhabitants love cant. It's more than likely the murderer doesn't belong to our tribe and has come from outside. If the murderer is an outsider, the Canters are top of my list; as far as we know, they are the only prehistoric community round here. After I informed Ethelred of my conclusions, our chief decided to send out a fact-finding mission.

Ethelred, Rufus, Alfred and yours truly went to Canterbury. Initially, we were on tenterhooks, given that the Canters are practising cannibals (endocannibals is the term they use) and we were afraid they'd gobble us up before we could explain why we'd come. In the end, our fears were unfounded. The Canterbury Neanderthals are amazingly hospitable and gave us a first-rate welcome, all things being equal. They even invited us to wash in a green bath of aromatic herbs, a form of ritual ablution, but as water is not our favourite element we politely refused the bath, claiming our beliefs forbade us to wash and we were there on business. After the typical exchange of presents – an oval stone for a round one, a trefoil for an ammonite – we told Penda, their chief, what had happened in our cave and of our suspicions. He was adamant in his response.

"How on earth could the murderer be a Canter if, as you say, nobody tucked into the corpses? You know we are cannibals!" he grimaced, visibly annoyed.

"Yes, but you always reckon you practise endocannibalism, I mean you only eat your own ..." I retaliated.

"In fact, we like a little bit of this and a little bit of that ..." Penda confessed rather reluctantly. "However, we use more sophisticated tools and don't go around killing people with rocks, like you do. For God's sake, if it had been one of us, he'd have used an axe, not a boulder!"

"True enough," I acquiesced.

"Right, let's be off then!" roared Ethelred, springing to his feet. "That's all cleared up, Penda, we won't bother you any more. Do forgive us for burdening you with all our woes. Some individuals," he added, giving me a withering look, "think they are real bloody *sapiens sapiens* ..."

"Don't worry," said Penda knowingly. "Weeds prosper wherever."

We walked back in silence, our tails between our legs (not merely metaphorically in Alfred's case). Back in our cave, I got a tongue-lashing and savaging I couldn't dodge. Ethelred and Rufus were livid and shouted at me in front of the women.

"We were made to look like complete fools!" Rufus spat in my face. "I don't know what the fucking use such a brainbox is if you never get it right!"

"To err is only human," I answered meekly.

"Come on, Mycroft, stop being such a Sherlock and get cracking. See if you can invent the axe!" added Ethelred. "We were made to look like a bunch of yokels!"

"All right, I'll see what I can do in the morning," I agreed.

I had no choice but to discount the outsider theory and concentrate on the inhabitants of our cave, because if the Canters are innocent, the guilty party must be one of us. After ruminating a while, waiting for the women to serve tea, I thought I'd better concentrate on discovering what the three victims, namely Athelstan, Beowulf and Lackland, had had in common, and I reached the following conclusions: a) all three were male; b) all three were hunters; c) none was immortal. Apart from that I drew a blank and couldn't establish a motive, because the deceased were all beautiful people. Strictly in terms of their characters, I mean.

After tea, while getting ready for my nap, I thought it would be worth my while to create a psychological profile of the murderer and see if I could eliminate any suspects. The results were disappointing: the only conclusion I drew was that the guilty man is someone who can wield a rock. I could discount the children and Offa, who's armless because a bear ate his arms one day while he was taking a siesta under a pile of branches by the cave. Not counting the three who have already passed away, there remain some fifty-three suspects, because I wouldn't want to leave the women out or they'd be furious and accuse me of being a male chauvinist pig. Fifty-three suspects are a lot, but it's better than nothing.

In any case, I needed to shorten my list. I retraced my steps, recalling how I'd established, quite reasonably, that the murderer must be a cold, calculating, intelligent fellow. Naturally, that led me automatically to eliminate women and children from my enquiry. I reviewed the list of males in the tribe and was basically unable to identify a single one worthy of the epithet of "intelligent". Once more, the finger of suspicion points at me: I don't have an alibi and am the only Neanderthal in the group whose neurons function at all. Moreover, I'm a cold customer and the only one able to calculate within a reasonably small margin of error how many tribal males are left now three have bitten the dust. I plucked up my courage and accepted the evidence: no doubt about it, I'm the murderer.

"I've solved the case," I told Ethelred, who was busy carving up a mammoth. "After examining the facts, I've reached the conclusion that I did it."

"What do you mean?" reacted Ethelred, putting the mammoth to one side and glowering at me.

"How often have I said to you that when you have eliminated the impossible, whatever remains, *however improbable*, must be the truth?" I declared. "Ethelred, I am the murderer."

"Mycroft, cut the crap!" thundered Ethelred, punching a rock and breaking a couple of bones in his left hand. "How the hell could you have killed them if you faint at the sight of a drop of blood …?"

"True enough. I'd forgotten."

"So, get on with it. If you don't solve this case, none of us will get any shut-eye and you're up for immolation. You do know that, don't you?"

"No, I didn't. It's news to me."

"Well, I had the idea a while back. We voted on the motion and it was passed *nem. con.* Sorry, I forgot to pass the news on."

"Fair enough."

I have the impression I'm miscuing this investigation. From the start I've focused on *who*, but perhaps if I concentrate on *why* the answer will come just like that. Why were Rufus, Beowulf and Athelstan in particular picked for the chop? What's the motive lurking behind their deaths? Who stands to gain?

There's one aspect that Lackland highlighted, and it may be worth consideration. All the males of the tribe are stressed out by the murders but the women, on the contrary, are as cool as cucumbers, as if the serial killer thing doesn't affect them. Not even Matilda, the matriarch of the group, seems the least worried by the fact we have a head-smashing psychopath in the cave. This makes me wonder. What can't I see? What am I missing?

We all know women have a secret: what they do to get pregnant. Do they swallow on the sly a magic root we know nothing about? Do they hoard their farts, inflate their bellies and thus create a child inside themselves? All us males are obsessed with procreation, because however much we bluster on our weekend binges, the females sit in the driving seat. If we could crack the secret behind pregnancy, the power they exert over us would evaporate. Can't you tidy the cave? You've pissed up the wrong tree! The meat was tough again! They treat us like dummies, and on the pretext that they have to suckle their babes they dispatch us to get rid of the rubbish and hunt wild animals, which means we often return to the cave missing a companion or short of a limb. But there's no way we can find out how the buggers do it.

The day before his head was smashed in, Lackland announced he'd found out their big secret: females get pregnant thanks to our white wee-wee. Of course, this is pure idiocy, and apart from Athelstan and Rufus, who are the most credulous of men, none of us gave it a second thought. I mean, if male wee-wee is what gets women pregnant … the goats and hens in the corral would also be bringing kids into the world! Those poor chaps are so simple-minded!

Even though I don't think the women's secret is connected to the homicides, I decided to have a word with Matilda because all this is making me feel uneasy. I told her my doubts and she immediately reassured me.

"Mycroft, don't get your knickers in a twist, I beg you."

"It's just that you don't seem scared of the psychopath in the cave. At the very least, it's a little odd …"

"So you want to be the next to appear one morning with his head smashed in, do you?" she asked, picking up a rock.

"Of course I don't … But if I don't find the guilty party, they're going to immolate me at the crack of dawn. You know how pernickety old Ethelred is …"

"Sit down and listen to me, then," she said with a sigh. "This is what you must tell Ethelred and his band of rogues."

As Matilda isn't short of spunk and is more than able to send an adult male flying from one end of the cave to another, I sat obediently by her side and listened to her most rational explanations. Given her excellent aim when sling-hunting bats, I found her arguments entirely persuasive. I immediately went to see Ethelred to tell him a second time that I'd solved the case.

"Beowulf, Lackland and Athelstan were punished by the gods because they discovered something they weren't supposed to know," I affirmed smugly.

"And what might that be?" asked Ethelred offhandedly.

"The women's secret. The child thing …"

"Oh …!" Ethelred scratched his private parts with his nails and out jumped a couple of fleas. "And who the fuck might these gods be?"

"Gods are superior beings who rule the universe," I answered, making it up as I went along. "They are eternal, almighty and immortal. From up in the sky where they live, they see all and know all."

"How do *you* know?" he enquired, looking at me like a dead fish.

"I had a vision in my dreams. I was told that if we stop trying to find out what women do to get with child there will be no more deaths."

"What good news!" exclaimed Ethelred, squashing another flea. "Case closed! Now let's dine. I'm so hungry I could eat a diplodocus!"

And added, with a grin, winking his only eye at me, "If they weren't extinct, I mean …"

I can't complain. Today I've solved three murders and in one fell swoop invented prophecies, gods and oneiromancy. And saved my own skin into the bargain. The only thing worrying me now is that henceforth everybody will be badgering me to interpret their dreams and will have the cheek to want me to do it for nothing. I can see it now: "I'm having erotic dreams about my mother or dream of killing my father." Or, "Yesterday I dreamt Cnut's menhir was bigger than mine …" You know, perhaps I should consider inventing psychoanalysis. It's not as if I have anything better to do.

The Son-in-Law

The *mossos* came this morning. I'd been expecting them
for days.

When I opened the door, they were still out of breath.
That's nothing unusual. Visitors all get to my attic flat
on the seventh floor on their last legs: there's no lift.
The stairs are steep and they're an effort to climb, and
instead of taking it calmly, like Carmeta and me, they
must have pelted up like lunatics. I reckon their uniforms
will have set the neighbours' tongues wagging; there are
a number of pensioners with nothing better to do than
look through their spyholes at my staircase. I only hope
the *mossos* don't decide to question them, because my
neighbours love to stir things. In any case, I don't think
they suspect any funny business.

There was a man and a woman, nice and polite they
were, and she was much younger. My hair was tangled,
I wasn't made up and was wearing the horrible sky-blue
polyester bathrobe and granny slippers I'd taken the
precaution of buying a few days ago at one of the stalls
in the Ninot market. The bathrobe is very similar to the

one worn by Conxita, the eighty-year-old on the second floor, but it looked too new so I put it through the washing machine several times the day before yesterday so it was more like an old rag, which is how I wanted it to look. Now the bathrobe was frayed and flecked with little bobbles of fluff, and, to round off the effect, I spilled a cup of coffee I was drinking over my bust. The woman tactfully scrutinized me from head to toe, dwelling on the stains and dishevelled hair, and I was really lucky one of the police belonged to the female sex since we ladies take much more notice of the small details than the menfolk do. She seemed very on the ball and I trust she drew her own conclusions from my shabby appearance.

Her colleague, fortyish and with Paul Newman's eyes, was the one in charge. He introduced himself very nicely, asked me if I was who I am and said he just had a few questions he wanted to ask. A routine enquiry, he added, smiling soothingly. I'd nothing to worry about. I adopted the astonished expression I'd been rehearsing for days in front of the mirror and invited them into the dining room.

As they followed me down the passage, I made sure I gave them the impression I was a frail, sickly old dear struggling to walk and draw breath. I exaggerated, because I'm pretty sprightly for my age and, thank God, I'm not in bad health, although I tried to imitate the way Carmeta walks, dragging my feet at the speed of a turtle, as if every bone in my body was aching. Both homed in on the sacks of cement, the tins of paint and workmen's tools that are still in the passage, and asked me if I was having building work done. I told them the truth: that after all that rain, the kitchen ceiling had collapsed and it had been a real mess.

"If only you'd seen it …! You'd have thought a bomb had dropped!" I told them with a sigh. "And it was so lucky I was watching the TV in the dining room …!"

The young policewoman nodded sympathetically and said that was the drawback with top-floor flats, though an attic has lots of advantages because you get a terrace and plenty of light. "What's more," she added shyly, "with all the traffic there is in the Eixample, you don't hear the noise from the cars or breathe in so many fumes." I agreed and told her a bit about what the Eixample was like almost fifty years ago, when Andreu and I first came to live here.

Visibly on edge, her colleague interrupted and asked me if I'd heard anything from my son-in-law. I adopted my slightly senile expression again and said I hadn't.

The policeman persisted. He wanted to know the last time I'd seen Marçal and if I'd spoken to him by phone. I told him as ingenuously as I could that I'd not heard from him for some time, and politely enquired why he was asking.

"He disappeared a week ago and his family think something untoward may have happened. That's why we're talking to everyone who knows him," he replied softly. "I don't suppose you know where he's got to, do you?"

"Who?" I said, pretending to be in the early stages of Alzheimer's.

"Your son-in-law."

"Marçal?"

"Yes, Marçal."

"Sorry … What was it you just asked me?"

Like those old people who really don't cotton on, I changed the subject and asked them if they'd like a drink – a coffee, an infusion or something stronger. When they asked me if I knew that he and my little girl were negotiating a divorce and if I was aware my son-in-law had a restraining order in force because she'd reported him for physical abuse, I simply looked at the floor and shrugged my shoulders. Reluctantly, I confessed I suspected things weren't going too well.

"But all married couples have problems … I didn't want to harp on about theirs," I said, adding, "Nowadays women don't have the patience … In my time …"

I didn't finish my sentence. There was no need. The young policewoman looked at me affectionately and gave one of those condescending smiles liberated young females of today reserve for us old wrinklies with antiquated ideas. Out of the corner of one eye, I registered that she'd had a French manicure and wore a wedding ring. To judge by her pink cheeks and smiley expression, the young woman must still be in the honeymoon period.

Before they could start grilling me about Marçal and his relationship with Marta again, I began to gabble on about stuff that was totally unrelated, playing the part of an old dear who lives by herself, has nobody to talk to and spends her day sitting on her sofa in front of the

TV watching programmes she doesn't understand. My grousing made them uneasy, and the man finally glanced at his watch and said they ought to be leaving. Their visit (you couldn't really call it an interrogation) had lasted less than ten minutes. When they were saying goodbye, they repeated that I shouldn't worry. That it was probably just a misunderstanding.

Marta, my little girl, will soon be thirty-six. I'm seventy-four, and it's no secret that Andreu and I were getting on when I got pregnant with Marta. Nowadays it's quite normal to have your first baby at forty, but it wasn't in my day. If you didn't have a bun in the oven before you turned thirty, people scowled at you, as if it was a sin not to have children. The kindest comment they'd make was that you weren't up to it. If you were married and child-less, you suddenly became defective.

Marta is an only child. As she was such a latecomer, the poor dear didn't have a brother or sister. Apart from Carmeta and Ramon, who are kind of substitute aunt and uncle, my little girl doesn't have any real ones, or cousins for that matter. From the day we buried her father, may he rest in peace, Marta's only had Carmeta and me; you can hardly count Ramon, Carmeta's husband, since he had his stroke. Carmen has to feed him with some sort of puree she buys at the chemists that she administers with a syringe through a rubber tube that goes in through his nose and down to his stomach, a torture that's simply prolonging his agony because his doctors say he'll never recover. They insisted to Carmeta that Ramon isn't suffering, though we spend the whole blessed day with him and aren't so sure about that.

Carmeta's the same age as me, and, though I can't complain about my health, she's rather the worse for wear. A cancer she can't see the back of. She and Ramon didn't have children, and both doted on Marta like an aunt and uncle from the day she was born. My daughter loves them, and they love her. If it hadn't been for his stroke, I'd cross my heart and swear Ramon would have rearranged my son-in-law's face and things would have turned out differently.

A pity none of us was in the know a year ago.

We were completely in the dark.

Even though we sometimes said our little girl seemed to be behaving a bit strangely. Sluggishly. As if she were unhappy. But we all have our off days, don't we?

Our little girl put on a brave front. Partly because she didn't want us to worry, and partly because she was embarrassed to acknowledge that her husband beat her. If I'd never decided to buy some pastries and pay her a visit one day after accompanying Carmeta to her chemo session, I expect we'd still be none the wiser and it would be life as usual.

That morning, when Marta opened the door barricaded behind a pair of huge sunglasses, our alarm bells immediately started ringing. Something was amiss. She pretended she had conjunctivitis to justify the dark glasses indoors, but Carmeta, who's a suspicious sort, didn't swallow that and snatched them from her face. Our hearts missed several beats when we saw that black eye lurking under layers of make-up.

At first she denied it. Carmeta and I are no fools and applied the third degree, and she finally caved in. In floods of tears she confessed that her husband drank too much and beat her now and again. A punch, a slap, a shove … When he calmed down, he'd put it down to stress at work. He'd also say he would kill her if she ever told anyone.

I saw a bruise on my little girl's left arm and told her to strip off. The poor thing couldn't bring herself to say no and agreed, reluctantly. Then Carmeta and I burst into tears. Our darling Marta was black and blue all over. From that day on we never referred to him by his name again. My son-in-law became the Animal, the Son of a Bitch or the Bastard. We got weaving. We persuaded Marta to report him, and the three of us went to see a lawyer. Marta was afraid nobody would believe her and that the judge would take her child away, but the lawyer did a good job of reassuring her and, in the end, made a start on the paperwork. And it was true: with his executive suits and silk ties, the Bastard seemed like a normal person.

A cunt of a normal person who beat his wife and threatened to kill her.

And our little girl, quite naturally, was scared.

But now she had us on her side.

*

The Bastard went to live with his sister and disappeared from our lives for months. Marta, who'd been reduced to skin and bones by all the unpleasantness, even began to put on weight. Until one evening he appeared out of the blue at her place and said he was going to kill her.

It was only a matter of time.

Depending on his patience.

And Carmeta suddenly saw the light.

No well-intentioned law could protect Marta. If he put his mind to it, the Bastard would sooner or later do the evil deed. As he said, it was only a matter of time. A matter of waiting until one of us lowered her guard or the judge decided there were more serious cases to see to and that our little girl no longer needed protection. That she could manage on her own.

It's not hard to intimidate someone. Or to kill them.

And, in the meantime, the Bastard would ruin her life.

Hers and everybody else's.

It's a piece of luck I have an attic flat and that it's got a terrace. The woman *mosso* was right. Attics can be very inconvenient, but they have lots of advantages. And if you don't agree, just ask the Bastard.

Andreu and I rented this flat on the Eixample just before we got married, and the only thing my husband insisted on when we were courting and looking for a flat was that it should have a small terrace. My parents didn't have a terrace because we lived on the third floor, but when the weather was good we'd go up to the flat roof and enjoy the cool of evening and gossip with the neighbours. I'd go there with my friends in the summer. We'd put our swimsuits on, lay our beach towels on the red tiles and imitate the film stars in our magazines, listening to the radio and drinking fizzy lemonade or tepid Coca-Cola, pretending it was Martini. Then we'd have to fight off sunstroke with aspirins, water packs and vinegar, but it was worth it. When you're young, there's a solution to everything.

It's not that my little terrace is any great shakes. All the same, twenty-two square metres are enough for a pine, a lemon and an orange tree, a magnolia, a decent-sized jasmine and a bougainvillea, not to mention the dozens of pots of roses, petunias, daisies and chrysanthemums I've put in every cranny. When Andreu and I set foot on it for the first time, I could hardly imagine how providential this little terrace would turn out to be.

Because I don't know how I could have helped my little girl without it.

And I reckon that's what a mother's for: to be around to give a helping hand to her children when they've got problems. Whether they like it or not.

It was Carmeta who came up with the solution. She's always been very imaginative. The terrace and the kitchen that the downpour had ruined gave her the idea, and no sooner was it said than done. Neither of us was prepared to wait with arms folded while my little girl was left at the mercy of an obsolete legal system and a lunatic who wanted to bump her off. We had to do something, and do it quick, before we lost our nerve. As Carmeta said, a stitch in time saves nine.

I called the Bastard on his mobile a couple of weeks ago from a phone box and told him we needed to have a chat. I persuaded him by saying I had to tell him about a new development that would make Marta slow up on the divorce, and, as I knew he was short of cash because he was drinking a lot and had got the sack, I added that I wanted to give him a present of a weekend away with Marta. Three or four days in a good hotel with a swimming pool, all expenses paid, would help them make peace, I told him. My call and sudden interest in saving their marriage took him by surprise, but, as Carmeta had anticipated, the financial bait hooked him.

Early the next morning, Carmeta came to my flat carrying a sports bag. Her face looked haggard and she confessed she'd had a bad night. I told her I could ring the Bastard and give him an excuse if she'd rather leave it for another day, but she'd hear none of it. The tranquillizers she'd taken were beginning to take effect and she already felt slightly better, or so she said.

"What do you reckon? Should we have a little drop of something to put us in the mood?" I suggested hesitantly.

"No alcohol!" replied Carmeta, most professionally. "What we need are anti-stress pills. We're far too nervy."

Out of her bag, Carmeta took the antidepressants that the doctor had prescribed after telling her she had cancer, and offered me one. As she's the expert when it comes to pills, I meekly swallowed it and said nothing. Out of the corner of my eye I noted that she took two. I went to the kitchen and made two cups of tea while Carmeta changed her clothes in the bedroom. She had brought an old tracksuit top and slippers. I was also wearing old clothes that would have to be thrown away.

The Bastard arrived around eleven. Grudgingly, I pecked him on both cheeks and led him into the dining room. With a studiedly senile smile, I offered him a cognac, which the idiot accepted in a flash while he lolled on the sofa. I seized the opportunity to go into the kitchen.

"Marçal!" I shouted, trying to ensure I didn't sound rude. "Could you help me get the bottle of cognac from the top shelf. I can't reach it ..."

I'd left the knife under a tea towel on the kitchen top, and Carmeta was skulking behind the door, holding her breath. As soon as I heard his footsteps, I shut the window and switched on the radio.

The second Marçal stepped into the kitchen, Carmeta stuck the carving knife into the small of his back. The attack took him by surprise and he started howling. Before he had time to react, I grabbed the knife from under the tea towel and stuck it in violently. Blood spurted from his neck and through the air like a liquid streamer, splashing everywhere.

Still screaming, the Animal lifted his hands to his neck in an attempt to stop the haemorrhaging, but from the way the blood was bubbling out, I knew he had no chance. I'd stuck it right in his carotid artery, and that thrust, driven by a mother's fury, was a death sentence.

He collapsed in under a minute. Carmeta and I left him agonizing on the kitchen floor and went into the bathroom. We washed our hands and faces, changed our blood-soaked tops and went into the dining room. We wanted the Bastard to die alone, like a dog. And he did. A Beatles song on the radio drowned out his cries.

By the time we went back to the kitchen, my son-in-law was dead. The floor had turned into a red puddle and was awash with blood. The Son of a Bitch had left one hell of a mess. We pulled on rubber gloves, grabbed the bucket and cloth and started cleaning up. The two of us were at it for a good hour, but even so it still wasn't spotless.

After checking his body had stopped bleeding, we stripped him and put his clothes in the washer on a cool cycle, adding a squirt of one of those stain removers advertised on the TV. We wiped him a bit with the cloth. Then I took some rolls of bandage from a drawer and Carmeta and I bound him like a mummy. As we were intending to cut him into small chunks, we thought it would be less unpleasant for us if he were bandaged. I started on his head and Carmeta on his feet.

It took us ages because the Bastard weighed more than ninety kilos and wasn't easy to lift. When we'd finished our bandaging, we left him and went back to the dining room. The effort had left us exhausted. We saw it was lunchtime, and though neither Carmeta nor I were hungry, we behaved ourselves, ate a banana and drank a glass of sugared water to re-energize. We also took another antidepressant each. Carmeta, who was worn out, dozed off straight away, and I decided to let her sleep and take a nap myself. When she woke up, she swallowed another batch of tranquillizers and we both returned to our task. Our day wasn't over yet.

Carmeta went to fetch the electric saw and brought it into the kitchen. Luckily one of her neighbours is into DIY and the storeroom in her building isn't locked. We pulled our rubber gloves back on and plugged in the saw, which worked perfectly. We cut his head off first and placed it whole inside a rubbish bag, and then his arms and legs, all in small chunks. We divided the pieces among different sacks and left his torso till last. As that's where the entrails are, Carmeta and I thought it would be best to empty them out before starting to reduce the eventual mess.

I took my courage into my own hands and very carefully made an incision from the top to the bottom of his mutilated corpse, trying to tear only the skin. I must have burst his gut, because all of a sudden a horrific stink filled the kitchen and I had to open the window and squirt air freshener around. Each of us pulled on one side of his torso and succeeded in separating his ribs and wrenching out his heart and lungs. His heart slipped out of Carmeta's grasp, and the moment it slopped on the ground I started to retch and vomit. As I'd practically been fasting I only brought up yellow bile, but I felt queasy and my stomach was churning.

Carmeta rushed me into the dining room and forced me to stretch out on the floor with my legs in the air. When she saw that I was showing signs of life again, she went back to the kitchen.

"Don't move. I'll gut the Son of a Bitch," she said.

There was still some sun on the terrace. The pale rays of spring barely gave out any heat but were a pleasant reminder of other, happier evenings when with Andreu (may he rest in peace), Carmeta and Ramon we'd rustle up a bread, tomato and mountain ham snack and stay up there late into the night chatting about this and that, never imagining that one day this small terrace of mine, with its views of Montjuïc and its flowerpots, would be an improvised cemetery. Necessity is the mother of invention, or so they say.

We buried the head next to the lemon tree, the one with the biggest pot, and stuffed his hands and feet into the ceramic pot with the pine tree. We stuck his entrails in with the magnolia, his heart in with the bougainvillea and his liver in with the orange tree, and divided the rest up among the remaining pots, taking care not to damage the flowers. We'd scarcely finished when we realized there were still seven or eight pieces of meat in a bag and we had no receptacles left, but after toiling the whole day, at that time of night we were fit to drop, so I suggested to Carmeta that we should wrap them in foil and put them in the freezer, adding, "We'll think of something tomorrow after we've had a rest."

Carmeta looked in a bad way again. Although she wasn't complaining, her grimaces showed the pain she was in. I helped her shower and wash her hair, and switched on a washload of tops, towels and cloths we'd used to clean up the kitchen. The foam in the washing machine turned pink.

Ignoring her protests, I accompanied her home, and on the way threw the Bastard's clothes into a rubbish container. Carmeta could hardly stand up straight, so I made her a glass of hot milk and forced her to eat some biscuits before going to bed. I waited until she fell asleep and, while she snored, I changed Ramon's nappy and gave him his supper. Just before I left, as I was giving him a kiss on the forehead, I thought how sooner or later we'd have to do something to help him too. Good people don't deserve to end up like that.

The minute I opened the door to my flat, I realized that if I continued on an empty stomach, without any food input, my blood pressure would take a dive and I'd faint. In the morning, before the Bastard arrived, I'd taken the precaution of leaving some sandwiches in the dining room so as not to have to go back into the kitchen. As my stomach was slightly queasy, I had a couple of spoons of syrup and ate a ham sandwich and an apple while watching the news. The sandwich and apple went down well, and I was soon asleep on the sofa in front of the TV that was still on. That night, unlike the others, I didn't have a nightmare.

The next morning I got up early and spent the day giving the rest of the flat a thorough clean. Although they say bleach doesn't remove traces of blood, I'd bet anything you like that if the police decided to investigate they wouldn't find a scrap of evidence. I took a mid-morning break and first phoned Marta, who was at work, and then Carmeta, who'd got up and was feeling better. I continued cleaning. When I finished, it was past four and my back was aching.

I took the tops, cleaning cloths and towels out of the dryer, put everything into plastic sacks and went out. I threw the sacks into four different containers on my way to Ramon and Carmeta's. Carmeta was in much better spirits and was waiting for me with a bottle of cava in the fridge, which we drank while we kept Ramon company.

The builders came the following day and gutted the kitchen with their hammers. They also chipped out the wall and floor tiles. They worked at it a good two weeks, and now I have a new ceiling, designer tiles and a built-in kitchen. The tiles and cupboards are nothing out of the ordinary because they were bought in a sale, but altogether it looks really good.

I know I must keep my lips sealed and that I can't tell my little girl not to worry, that the Bastard won't ever lay his hands on her again. Marta knows nothing. Nothing at all. She's still very young, and God knows how she'd react if she knew what Carmeta and I had done. Besides, what with her kid and her work, Marta has enough headaches, and it would be the last straw if she had to cope with moral dilemmas or stupid remorse. So mum's definitely the word! If what we did was wrong, Carmeta says, we'll settle our account in the world beyond, with whoever.

Some girls from our yoga group are coming to supper tomorrow. We'll take advantage of the good weather and dine on the terrace. Just in case, I've bought a good supply of incense sticks, I mean, just in case the Bastard starts to get smelly and sour our meal. As Carmeta has to start another round of chemo and is leaving the class, it'll be a kind of farewell party. I've also dropped out of the class, because from tomorrow I'm going to live at her place for a while. When she starts being sick and feeling like a dishrag, Carmeta will need someone to accompany her to hospital and lend her a helping hand with Ramon.

We both know she's not got much time left. She knows and I know, so there's no need to mention it. Nonetheless, tomorrow's farewell will be a whale of party: we'll eat and drink until our livers give out on us. It's not our style to turn tragic, and even less so when we've both got one foot on the other side. What's coming our way is coming.

I live very near the Ninot market, where I shop every day. I like to look around the stalls and gossip with the saleswomen and locals from the neighbourhood. As I'm there daily and never use the freezer, I'd completely forgotten the packets that were still there. That morning, the visit by the police had reminded me I must do something about that, and I rang Carmeta. I told her I was thinking of going to the florists and buying some earth and a couple of big pots.

"Forget about the pots!" Carmeta retorted. "Go to the Ninot and see if you can buy some spongy mushrooms and fairy rings. And buy garlic and onions as well. Tomorrow," she added in an authoritarian tone, "we shall eat roast pork and spring mushrooms!"

Initially I objected, mostly on behalf of the other girls. But, in the cold light of day, I have to agree it's not a bad solution.

Still Life No. 41

I've been sacked. It happened this morning. The chief executive summoned me to his office and said he was sorry but the minister had decided to relieve me of my post. He said the scandal had gone too far, and he couldn't brush it under the carpet. I tried to defend myself, but realized it was hopeless. There was no way he was going to reverse his decision. He dismissed me, my tears welled up and I went to the bathroom for a good cry.

It's unfair. Anyone could have made the same error. And I mean anyone. In fact, nobody noticed the day the exhibition opened. Or the day after. A week went by before the mistake was spotted. Because it *was* a mistake, and a bad one at that.

I wasn't to blame for what happened. No way. And the proof is that the police who arrested me in the first instance let me go scot-free after a couple of days. It was obvious I'd done everything in good faith and that it had simply been one big gaffe. Maybe I was a little naive – "incompetent" was the word the Minister of Culture actually used – but naivety and incompetence are hardly crimes. I reckon everyone has a right to make mistakes. What really pisses me off is that I won't find another job in the art world for a good long time as a result of this ridiculous business.

They say that at the end of the day it was my responsibility and that's why they're giving me the push, but it's obvious they need a scapegoat. They're a bunch of chauvinist pigs. They gave me the option of resigning rather than being sacked. I accepted, naturally.

There was only one day to go until the inauguration of the exhibition and I was nervous, as you can imagine. If you have ever curated an exhibition, you'll know what I mean. I'd just started in my post as director of the MUAA and it was the first big exhibition I had organized by myself. I was nervous, but also very excited, and so happy, I can tell you. A mere twenty-six years old and here I was about to enter the city's art scene through the front door, because it's no mean feat to be Director of the Museum of Ultra-Avant-Garde Art. Absolutely not. Quite a few people would kill for a position like it, and though I knew every step I made would be scrutinized under a magnifying glass to see whether I triumphed or made a cock-up of things, I was convinced the exhibition would be a success and that I'd get my fair share of congratulations. And that *was* how it turned out. The launch was first-rate and the artworks and canapés mesmerized those invited in equal measure. They all said Eudald Mataplana was a great artist, and the catering firm I contracted belonged to a girlfriend I trusted completely. If you're going to do something, then do it well, I say.

As I told the police, I didn't choose the subject of the exhibition, let alone the pieces that were exhibited. The museum had been negotiating for two years with the artist's agent and I'd only just taken up my post as director. The tragic disappearance of my predecessor, who according to the official version died of a sudden heart attack, and according to the off-the-record account from an overdose of blue pills, was a real stroke of luck. One of the openings for an art history graduate is a post directing a museum or gallery; the deceased was an uncle of mine, and that coincidence really smoothed the path for me. When Uncle died, I'd already been working with him for a year and a half, and Daddy immediately rang the Minister to remind him of a thing or two. Obviously these posts aren't hereditary, but Daddy likes to see some return on the money he pays out every election time. Besides, competition for any decent post is so fierce nowadays it's hardly a mortal sin for a father to give his daughter a helping hand. Blood is thicker than water, and Daddy has so many contacts it would be criminal not to take advantage of one occasionally.

My uncle was an old friend and great admirer of Eudald Mataplana, and that explains why he decided to curate the exhibition himself. To tell the truth, I wasn't at all familiar with his work and I'd never met him personally, because contemporary art isn't my strong point and all my meetings had been with his agent.

I had a panic attack the day before the exhibition opened when I realized there weren't forty works, as stated in the agreement signed by the museum, but forty-one.

"What the hell's *that* doing there?" I asked, put out, when I saw the piece in the main room.

"We don't know where to put it," the installers replied, deadpan.

I took another look at the sculpture and thought hard. I didn't think I'd ever seen it before. After thoroughly reviewing my list, I concluded that the piece wasn't part of the selection made for our exhibition. It was an extra. But there it was, and, what's more, it was no small item. I reflected for a while, then decided to ring the artist and seek his advice.

Eudald Mataplana wasn't answering his house phone or his mobile. "Typical bloody artist, out on the tiles till late and then sleeping it off in the morning!" I raged enviously. I left a message on his answering machine, not thinking for one moment that he'd ever hear it, and pondered what to do next. I knew it was a waste of time to try to speak to his agent, because he'd be flying over an ocean at that point. And Uncle was dead, so I didn't know who I could turn to. I started to feel nervous. It wasn't yet midday and I had to reach a decision on whether to send the item back to the artist's studio (I'd have to phone the moving firm, talk to the insurance company, change the budget ...) or discreetly shift it down into the basement. The item wasn't in the catalogue, and it put me on the spot.

"What do I do now?" I asked my secretary in a fit of despair. "I've got an appointment at the hairdresser's and then at the beautician's. We launch the show tomorrow and I've still got to fetch the dress that they're adjusting —"

"If they've sent it, it means they want it in the exhibition," she said in her very matter-of-fact way. "Find a place for it and don't worry so much. After all, it's only one more sculpture."

And that's just what I did. I told the installers to erect a dais in the centre of the main room, the only free space left for a work of that size, and told them to put it right there. The title for the work wasn't a problem, as the names were all virtually the same: *Still Life No.1*, *Still Life No. 2*, *Still Life No. 3* … I printed out a label on my computer with the title *Still Life No. 41* and placed it in front of the piece that really took your breath away.

Eudald Mataplana cultivated an oneiric-deconstructionist hyperrealism, with baroque touches that he injected with a high emotional charge. Or, to put it in plain English, he spent his time creating realistic sculptures on shocking themes to jolt his public out of their aesthetic comfort zones and provoke repulsion. I don't know why he did it, or why his work was so successful. The fact is, all his sculptures had as their leitmotifs degeneration, sickness and death in their most macabre forms: cats and dogs that had been run over, rotten fruit and withered flowers, battered children, women undergoing chemotherapy, decrepit elderly people, worm-infested skeletons … And to rub it in, the guy added odours to his sculptures, so his withered flowers stank of withered flowers, his sick women of hospitals and his old people of urine and excrement. They were subtle smells (you had to get up close to catch a whiff), but I found them all highly unpleasant, preferring to contemplate his works from afar.

My special interest, to be frank, is the Renaissance, and to be precise, the painting and sculpture of the Quattrocento: Donatello, Botticelli, Piero della Francesca … artists who have gone out of fashion. I've no real enthusiasm for modern art. I can't really see the point. Nonetheless, it was inevitable the contacts my uncle had with avant-garde artists would channel my career far away from my beloved Italians. Getting a post at the MUAA was a way to get noticed on the art scene and boost my CV, and one can't reject an opportunity like that when it comes served on a silver platter. Clearly I'm not a total illiterate in terms of contemporary art, and I don't want to justify my actions by pleading ignorance, but the avant-garde sensibility is so heterogeneous there's no way to categorize it or decide what criteria to use in its appreciation. If Uncle said Eudald Mataplana was good, I believed him. If his work wowed the viewing public, then even better.

I looked spectacular on the day of the launch. I'd lost four kilos and wore a cerise silk bodycon dress that had cost a bomb and sparked a lot of comment. The chief executive came, as did the Minister of Culture, the President of the Parliament and the mayor. Eudald Mataplana didn't, but his absence was no surprise because Eudald was a bit of an idiot and it was just like him to do that kind of thing. Some artists move heaven and earth to secure an interview or appear on TV, while others play hard to get and attract interviews that way, because they never normally grant them and claim they have a phobia when it comes to TV studios. Eudald Mataplana was one such artist: he organized a party and went AWOL; an exhibition of his work took place and he didn't bother to put in an appearance. In the end, everyone described him as a prickly character with a fondness for *enfant terrible* antics, and journalists frequently came to blows trying to get a statement, interview or photo out of him. The gossips said it was all part of a strategy dreamed up by his agent, but how could you tell? In this country, envy is the mother of all rumours.

Still Life No. 41 was the piece that received by far the most praise. Everyone agreed that the sculpture of a male corpse in the foetal position was easily the most accomplished. The critics praised it to the skies – what a masterpiece! what sensibility! – and it reduced the viewing public to silence. It was certainly the subtlest of all the exhibits, because the figure was clothed from head to foot and its eyes were hidden behind sunglasses. Nevertheless, the consensus was that the expression of grief glimpsed behind those glasses (by the way, they were fabulously expensive Armanis) was *incredibly* moving. Eudald Mataplana thus succeeded in rekindling his status as a cult figure for the country's most sophisticated elites.

As the days went by, big crowds came to see the exhibition. At times there were even long queues. We also began to notice that, with each day, the smell got stronger and stronger in the room where *Still Life No. 41* was on display, and that the sculpture's face and hands were changing shape and colour. Initially they were a marble white like the corpse depicted by Rembrandt in his *Anatomy Lesson of Dr Nicolaes Tulp*, but then they gradually turned a repugnant green and few people dared to look at them for long. After day three, the sculpture began to swell and stuck out its tongue. Everybody thought that was hilarious.

We thought, reasonably enough, that Eudald Mataplana had done it on purpose and that the strong smell and changes to the figure were the result of his absolute mastery of the raw materials; nobody, absolutely nobody, had anything but outright praise for the artist's audacity and technical prowess.

"Madame Director," said Sadurní, tapping on the door and walking into my office, "there is a gentleman here who would like to speak to you."

Sadurní is one of the museum security guards who were on duty that day.

"A gentleman?"

"A visitor. He says it's important and that if you won't see him he'll go straight to the police."

"If I must," I said with a deep sigh. "Tell him to come in. But you stay near the door, right, Sadurní?"

Most of the loonies who slip into museums are harmless enough, but one can't be too careful. When the man walked into my office, I asked him to leave the door ajar on the pretext that my air conditioning wasn't working. He introduced himself and said he was a doctor.

"What the hell do you think you are doing displaying that decomposing corpse in the main room?" he blasted.

I smiled at him. A pity I was on the verge of marriage, because the guy was gorgeous and I could have done with a little fling to break my boring routine. Anyway, the anecdote about the doctor who'd been fooled by the incomparable art of Eudald Mataplana would be good publicity for the exhibition, and I began mentally drawing up a press release describing our encounter.

"Don't worry," I replied, still smiling. "It's only a sculpture. And it's extremely well made."

"It is *not* a sculpture," the doctor replied solemnly. "It is a dead man."

"You are quite wrong, it *is* a sculpture," I assured him. "No need to worry."

"Sculptures do not suppurate liquids. Nor do they create a stink. And nor do they attract insects."

"Oh, that's all the invention of an artist who is simply a genius."

"Now, miss, I'm the doctor here, and —"

"Would you mind telling me what your field is?" I asked, showing that I was beginning to lose my temper.

I was actually delighted by his wrong-headedness and already relishing the pleasure I would derive from telling the story to my friends over cocktails that night.

"I am a psychiatrist. But I can assure you I recognize a dead man when I see one."

I smiled yet again. I'd always thought psychiatrists were fascinating. And I had never yet dated one.

"I quite understand if the sculpture has upset you. If you like, we could go for a coffee and talk about it … I'm Fefa, by the way," I added, holding my hand out to shake his.

"Please follow me," he insisted in an authoritarian tone. "You must see this for yourself."

At that moment in stepped Sadurní, who'd inevitably been listening to our exchange.

"I'm sorry, Madame Director. Forgive me for meddling in something that's none of my business, but I do think you should go and have a look. The room really stinks."

I sighed. All right, I'd see this joke through to the bitter end, then I'd have more material for my press release and more to gossip about with my friends. I got up from my extremely uncomfortable designer chair and accompanied them.

The museum had had no visitors that day. As soon as I entered the main room, I understood why.

"My God, it really does stink to high heaven…! And where have all these flies come from?"

"Corpses attract insects. And you're lucky you've got air conditioning!" the doctor replied, giving me a good, hard look up and down.

"I don't believe it. It can't be true," I said, shuddering.

"Take a close look. What do you see?"

"It's green … and black in some places. And the skin is covered in blebs …"

"I'm no expert," he said, straightening his glasses and staring surreptitiously down my cleavage, "but I would estimate that this man has been dead at least a week. Take a look – his epidermis has separated from his dermis and the gases have caused his stomach to expand. That's why he's so inflated."

"I think he's vomited too …" I mumbled.

"Miss, that's the fluid created by his decomposing internal organs that are then expelled through the nose and mouth."

"My God!" I exclaimed, jumping backwards. "There are maggots everywhere …!"

I don't remember any more, because I fainted at that point.

The police took less than a minute to identify the corpse, which carried an ID card: it was Eudald Mataplana. As his head was completely shaven and he was wearing sunglasses, no one had recognized him. No one had missed him either, which didn't mean very much because he was a man with few friends – you know, who you'd call *real* friends.

After finding no traces of blood, the police first concluded he must have had a massive heart attack. Their second theory was that it was a case of self-immolation:

he'd been out of his mind and decided to poison himself so that he could become one of his own exhibits. Their thinking had some logic to it, but both theories were wrong. When the autopsy was carried out, the pathologist discovered a tiny hole in his shirt and a small wound in his thorax.

"The police believe it was murder," I announced at the press conference I called, to which I wore a white dress and a very fetching pink foulard. "The assassin stuck a thin, cylindrical pin through the ribs and across the pericardium, perforating the heart. As the wound was so tiny, his own blood plugged it as it dried, and that's why there was no blood," I explained, putting on a brave face as I read word for word the notes I'd cribbed from my secretary, who'd had a fling with the pathologist and snaffled a copy of the autopsy report for me. I added, absolutely confident that everyone would understand my mistake: "I think it was quite reasonable for me not to realize it wasn't a sculpture, don't you agree?"

Well, no, they didn't, and the next day the newspapers crucified me. It was evident I'd been under pressure with the launch, got my knickers in a twist and made a big error of judgement. I should have sent the item down to the basement. But it was too late now to put that right.

They're now saying it was one of his students. The girl had got tired of Eudald Mataplana taking every opportunity to feel her up, and, in a rage, had stuck into him one of the steel pins she was attaching to *Still Life No. 17*, a life-sized sculpture of a sick woman weaving while sitting in a wheelchair. They found traces of blood on the pin, and the installers immediately identified the girl who'd helped them mount the work. She's currently in the slammer.

I really couldn't care less about the student, Eudald Mataplana, his sculptures or the whole fucking show. All I know is that I'm out of work and that Daddy's calls haven't helped this time because of all the fallout from the scandal hitting the headlines. Mummy says I should forget it, as my hands are already full with the preparations for my wedding and Cancún honeymoon, but then she belongs to another generation and doesn't understand it's hardly the done thing any more not to work outside the home. I'm not awfully enthusiastic about having to clock in every morning, but we modern women, even if we belong to the upper classes, have to work, or at least go through the motions of working. Daddy says I shouldn't worry, that as soon as things calm down he'll pick up his telephone again. I'm going to think of it as paid holidays, because I gather I have a right to unemployment benefit, even though I technically resigned.

As Daddy says to console me, I'm young and have a whole lifetime in front of me. When I get back from Cancún, we'll see how things are. For the moment, I have a coffee date with that psychiatrist, whose name is Lluís and who is *awfully* nice. And, you know, if I'm bored when I get back from honeymoon and can't find my kind of work, I can always go into politics. Become an MP or something of the sort. Who knows, I am renowned for my drive and might make Secretary of State. Or Minister of Culture … Yes, it would be great to be a minister of something. Though I'm not sure … If I were a minister, I'd have to live in Madrid. And it's very cold in Madrid in winter, and very hot in summer … And they don't have a beach … Or a Port Olímpic. Or ski slopes nearby. And Mummy would be terribly distraught if I upped and went to live that far away …!

Happy Families

2 February

A couple came to look at the house today. We're very hopeful. He must be around fifty (though he has worn well, it has to be said) and we reckoned she's a gorgeous thirty-five. We deduced from their conversation with the estate agent that they're newlyweds and that, even in these crisis-ridden times, they have no money problems whatsoever. Apparently they liked the mansion, and we really hope they take it on. If only they would, because we've been bored to death here ever since Santi went over a precipice in his Alfa Romeo and his children put the place up for sale. The situation is getting tense. If nobody buys the house soon, things are bound to take a turn for the worse.

Over recent years we've had several visitors who seemed interested, but today's couple gave out good vibrations. They really need a house. Of course, we don't like the idea of our mansion being in the hands of people who aren't family, but we can't do much about that. Santi's children, who prefer to live in Sant Cugat, are determined to sell come what may, and it's only a matter of time before they find a buyer, however much their father grumbles. Meanwhile, the cobwebs are having a field day and Anastase, who is allergic to dust, sneezes the whole day long.

The presence of new tenants would at least liven the place up. Ever since the house has been uninhabited, we've become a lethargic lot, always fighting amongst ourselves. But you said this, no, I said that, if this, if that … Nights are unbearably long when there's nobody to tease, and daytime is a dead loss. The prospect that somebody might once more walk these passageways, watch TV and frolic in the bedrooms has put us all in a good mood.

The wife's name is Jacqueline and she speaks with a foreign accent. After exploring the house from top to bottom, she said it was adorable and that, as it's so spacious, if they take it, she'll have a small gym built. She loved the idea of being able to organize big parties in the main reception room, and even praised the ambience in the garden (it's romantic, she reckons). In truth, no gardener has been near it in years, so it's wild and full of weeds. More like a jungle. Her husband and the estate agent smiled at each other but didn't contradict her.

Her husband is an Andreu and belongs to the Dalmau clan. He's as tall as a tree, and spent the whole time he visited the house thinking about laying his wife. He said the house and land were a pretty good investment and, as far as he was concerned, if she liked it, then full steam ahead. The beautiful Jacqueline, who dresses very fashionably, wrinkled her nose and said they shouldn't rush things. As the rich are always very hoity-toity, we took no notice.

Besides, Andreu is right: this house is a first-rate investment. Santi's children are prepared to sell it at a knock-down price just to get rid of it, even if for a mansion of this nature, on three floors, with eight bedrooms and twelve bathrooms (not forgetting the garden with its pond, arbour and Olympic swimming pool), knock-down still means loads. At the low end, around three million euros was the figure we heard them mention to the agent. Santi is pulling his hair out (metaphorically speaking) because he says the mansion is worth double that, but most of us here are desperate for them to buy. If only we could be so lucky this time.

7 February

The three came back this afternoon with an architect who gave the mansion a general survey. He found no serious structural problems and declared the house to be in excellent shape for its age. We already knew that, but it's good to have confirmation from an expert. The architect's presence has given us a boost, because it means the couple are really interested. Santi continues to be very annoyed and keeps cursing his children, but the rest of us can't keep our feet on the ground. Finally we'll have something to laugh about …!

You know, whatever people might say, a ghost's life in an uninhabited house is no great shakes.

Once you get accustomed to wailing, crossing through walls and coexisting with other ghosts, being a wandering soul in an empty house is the most tedious thing on earth. Flesh-and-blood people bring joy to our lives with their idiocies; and what's more, if they have a sense of humour and don't suffer from weak hearts, we can play little jokes on them now and then and piss ourselves laughing. All us ghosts love a bit of fun (as well as watching TV), even though we must take care to ensure the living don't die from the shock or run off scared.

In our case, we're fortunate, because we're a happy band of souls in purgatory and are good company. For better or worse, this family has seen more than its fair share of violent or premature deaths, the necessary prerequisites for becoming a ghost. We have this peculiar tendency not to die peacefully in our beds, and for a time the rumour did the rounds that the house was cursed and that was the reason for so many unfortunate occurrences. The unvarnished truth is that some us were unlucky, and others plain stupid.

In any case, despite being over the moon at the idea of the house being inhabited again, we're all agreed on one thing: not one of us wants to have to share eternity with a stranger. It's one thing for complete unknowns to settle in temporarily on the other side of the mirror and help us while away our time, but quite another for us to have to live with them forever and ever, amen. Fine as an emergency antidote to our boredom, but as Santi says with great common sense, eternity is a family matter, and no two ways about it!

The mansion dates from 1730 and is close to Tibidabo. Old Sebastià Molina, who lived on the Carrer del Pi in the city centre, had it built thinking that his family could spend August there, so it was originally conceived as a summer residence. At the end of the nineteenth century, the Molinas left the Old City to live on the right-hand side of the Eixample that at the time was very trendy, but, as the area soon began to go downhill, in 1929 Lluís decided to move all his family to the mansion on a permanent basis. When the army rebelled in 1936, Lluís recounts, many of their neighbours shut up their grand houses and went to live in the countryside to avoid confrontation with the lunatic anarchists of the FAI, but our family hung on heroically in Barcelona until the Francoist troops liberated the city. However, we're not all fascists, not by any stretch of the imagination. In the sixties, some of us were so radical we even joined the Communist Party.

Ever since old Molina built Villa Diana, it has been handed down from father to daughter and mother to son. It has never had a change of name, and isn't called Villa Diana because old Molina's wife was a Diana (in fact, she was an Engràcia), but to honour the Roman equivalent of the Greek goddess of the woods. As one can easily deduce from the name he chose to baptize the residence, Molina the patriarch was a Freemason.

Elisenda is all of a flutter at the possibility that we will soon have guests who watch television. As she was born in the eighteenth century and never saw it in her lifetime, she became an addict the moment she discovered the box, and doesn't miss a minute. The problem is that we ghosts can't watch TV if someone doesn't switch it on first; in other words, we've been disconnected from the world for eight years. What's the latest fashion, I wonder? How are Barça doing? As we have no up-to-date news, we kill time laying bets.

Elisenda and Anastase have spent the most time in the house; they died violently at the end of the eighteenth century. Elisenda is the granddaughter of Sebastià Molina and the only one who survived a plague epidemic that decimated the family. Elisenda was married to Bernat, an irritable, ruddy-cheeked, bushy-browed man of wealth, and Bernat sent Elisenda to the other side with Anastase when he discovered that his wife and lifelong friend were lovers. He found them in bed together one day, grabbed his hunting rifle and shot them on the spot. When she passed on, Elisenda was thirty-six and had given Bernat two children, and bachelor Anastase was forty-one.

Anastase, who is evil-minded, says that Bernat lost it when he saw his was bigger, but we all know how Anastase likes to brag. Elisenda was very lucky, because the bullet hit her heart and did very little visible damage, whereas Anastase was shot in the face and balls, which didn't leave him looking very pretty. Although you get used to him, it's quite a shock when you bump into him unexpectedly in a passageway. To avoid upsets, we insist he wears a cowbell.

Antoni is one of Elisenda's children, and he's with us too. This Antoni is Josep's father, and they've both been acting the ghost in Villa Diana for nigh on two hundred years. Josep was knifed to death by his twin brother Jaume, in a family row over which of them was the heir; their birth certificate had disappeared and nobody in the family remembered whether Josep or Jaume had been born first. The inheritance was very desirable, and in a wild outburst Jaume, who'd inherited his grandfather's moods, decided to do something about it. The knifing didn't amount to more than a few scratches, but Josep was unlucky and they became infected. As antibiotics had yet to be invented, all the doctor could do was sign his death certificate.

Antoni, Josep's father, died of a heart attack the moment he saw his favourite son receive that fratricidal stab. As he'd hitherto been very healthy and death left him unmarked, he's the ghost who is in best shape. Jaume was never imprisoned because the family kept it quiet, and he finally inherited the house and the factories his father had built in Manresa and Barcelona. He immediately married a bankrupt but toffee-nosed aristocrat who bore him a daughter, Carmeta. Like her mother, Carmeta only had one child, another Jaume, and this Jaume begat Margarida, who is consequently one of Antoni's great-granddaughters and one of the youngest ghosts prowling around the mansion.

Margarida made her entry at the sweet young age of twenty-three, at the end of the nineteenth century, as a result of amorous deceptions. My relative decided to commit suicide with arsenic, convinced someone would save her at the last minute and that her ex-fiancé would have a rethink, but she overdosed and died. She now accepts that her father was right when he said that her head was full of stuff and nonsense because she was reading too many novels. And, obviously, given that she's rather dim-witted, the idea of going to a chemist's and swallowing a few spoonfuls of poison wasn't her own. From then on, we banned Flaubert.

The proof that great-great-grandmother Mercedes (may she rest in peace) was right when she complained that the maids were a lazy lot and only cleaned lightly is poor Arnau, who was poisoned by his wife Violeta with the spare arsenic that had simply been left over and forgotten in the pantry. As Violeta was brighter than Margarida and poisoned her husband slowly and patiently, his death certificate states that the cause of death was chronic gastroenteritis, source unknown. Obviously, the doctor was no genius. The proof is that nobody ever suspected her.

The father of Violeta's second husband keeps Arnau company: Antoni-intestines, who came to live here when he was widowed. We call him Antoni-intestines to distinguish him from Antoni-heart-attack, Josep's father. As Antoni-intestines died when he was blown up by a bomb an anarchist threw into the stalls at the Liceu opera house, he now travels this world as best he can with his guts hanging out.

Lluís is the son of Violeta and her second husband, and is also a ghost. He and Paquita, who'd been in service with the family from the age of fourteen and was responsible for initiating the Molinas into the world of sex, had the bad luck to be at home when a bomb dropped by German pilots in the spring of 1937 hit its target and blew up the ceiling of the master bedroom. We never have got to the bottom of what they were both doing in bed at siesta time while Lluís's wife was visiting her sister in Gràcia. When the bomb dropped, Lluís was sixty-six and Paquita forty-two.

Eugenia is perhaps, of us all, the one who's to be pitied most. She also wears a cowbell. She was knocked down by a train in 1976 in Canet de Mar after she'd just left a protest concert. It's not easy to describe the state she was left in because the train that ran over her made a right mess. Her version is that it was very hot and she was on her way to the beach in the moonlight when she stumbled on the line in her rope sandals and gave the train driver no time to brake. Though she denies it, some people reckon she'd been smoking dope during the concert and was a bit fuzzy-headed. Be that as it may, she too is with us here purging her sins.

Despite the fact that Eugenia's accident was highly dramatic and made mincemeat of her, her head is in perfect shape because she was decapitated by the train and her head rolled intact down to the beach. Ever since, she has carried it under the only arm she has left. Eugenia is one of Lluís's great-granddaughters (the guy who was bombed), and, like many of us here, is one of the black sheep of the family. When she was buried, everybody agreed that my cousin would never have come good given the lifestyle she was leading.

Santi is the last member of the family who lived in this house, and has yet to come to terms with his status as a soul in purgatory. He was no chicken when he hurled himself and his Alfa Romeo over a precipice at two hundred and fifty an hour en route to the casino in Monte Carlo; his most outstanding virtues were his innate capacity to drink Cardhu without getting drunk and his total ignorance of what work was all about.

As for yours truly, I am Eugenia's cousin and have been a ghost since 1981. In my case, I died aged thirty-five in a rather silly fashion: from an overdose of adulterated heroin. I too never actually worked, but rather than polishing off the family inheritance in casinos on the Côte d'Azur like my nephew Santi, I was into the theatre, poetry and drugs. Frankly, I was a dead loss as an actor, a piss-poor poet and, as a druggy, ended my life as a piece of shit in a trendy club to the sound of a song by the Bee Gees, who, by the way, never wowed me. In such straits, I'd rather have passed away listening to Lou Reed or Janis

Joplin and not that sentimental claptrap, but as Eugenia, who has always had a rather mystical side to her, says, in this life you get what you deserve.

Jacqueline came back this morning accompanied by the estate agent and a very strange individual. Santi says he must be an interior designer. The man scrutinized every corner of the house and said it would be a lot of work but he'd do a good job. I imagine this means that they're going to buy the mansion and are planning to refurbish. As this kind of transaction takes time, we'll just have to be patient. In the meantime, we keep laying bets as to who's in government and who won the league.

7 March

After almost three weeks without any news, Jacqueline came back today with that oddball, whose name is Rafa. We discovered that the couple have finally bought the house and that Rafa isn't just an interior designer, as Santi suggested, but a guru who preaches a way-out religion. Jacqueline gave him a cheque and he promised to chase bad vibrations and evil spirits away from the house.

After drinking a cup of tea, Rafa took his shoes off and put on a white tunic that was rather tight on him. He immediately began lighting candles and distributing them throughout the house while he burned joss sticks and recited exorcisms in a language none of us could identify. We had to hide quickly in the small cupboard where they stored brooms and a bucket, because, although candles and exorcisms have no impact on us, the fumes are torture. Luckily, according to Elisenda, this kind of magic is very spectacular but short-lived.

From the very start, I'd thought the guy peculiar, but Santi reckons that's what interior designers are like.

10 March

We've been shut up in the cupboard for three days and still can't come out. We're very uncomfortable in here, accustomed as we are to having four hundred square metres to ourselves. Elisenda says that at most Rafa's spell might last for a week, and that we shouldn't despair.

All of us who still have fingers crossed them in the hope that our forebear is right.

14 March

We were finally able to leave the little cupboard this afternoon. The effects of the exorcism have faded and the house is now full of painters and builders. They're doing a full-scale refurbishment and have created a real pigsty. It doesn't seem the same house.

We gathered from Jacqueline's conversations with Rafa that Andreu is a financial tycoon and also rather tight-fisted. Jacqueline is his second wife, and Andreu's children can't stand her. We also found out that she was a fashion model who, years ago, trod the catwalks. That explains why she's so shapely.

It's fun to have mortals back and we're so happy. We're hoping that they'll employ an attractive young maid because the rich are mostly not at home and we ghosts must often make do with spying on the servants and pestering them.

2 May

They've finally finished the building work and brought the new furniture. Rafa, the man in the white tunic, returned and Elisenda, Paquita and Margarida rushed back into the little cupboard. This time, however, we were all safe and sound because he didn't fumigate. The fellow did lots of play-acting (I have to confess he's a better actor than I am), and simply explained how the furniture should be arranged according to the philosophy of feng shui. Jacqueline, who is rather simple-minded, was all excited.

The bad news is that we have discovered that there are now only two mirrors in the house. They have put one in Andreu's bathroom and the other in Jacqueline's. The mirror in Jacqueline's bathroom is full-length but is inside her cosmetics cupboard, so when the door is closed there might as well be no mirror. Santi says it's because they've found out that mirrors drain people's energy, although they don't yet know how because mirrors are made from sand and, in principle, have neither brains nor wills of their own. It's clearly a feng shui thing and not worth getting a headache over.

The mirror business is a bastard, however, because, as everybody knows, we ghosts use mirrors to change dimension, and they are indispensable. During the day, we're compelled to stay on the other side of the mirror and can't make contact with mortals, however much their exorcisms may impact on us in that phantom dimension where left and right are interchanged. We ghosts cannot enter the world of the living until midnight, and, to complicate matters, we can only do so through a mirror.

Until now, we each had our favourite. Eugenia and Elisenda always used the spectacular mirror in the entrance hall that had a hand-carved, gold-leaf frame, while Josep, Antoni and Paquita usually used the one in the dining room. Margarida preferred the small mirror in one of the guest bedrooms, the one decorated with maritime motifs, and Anastase and Antoni-intestines always came out of the ones in the main bedroom. Lluís and Santi had a preference for the mirror in the maid's bedroom, especially when the maid slept naked there in summer. Yours truly had always liked the small mirror in one corner of the library, by the chaise longue, that also had a gold-leaf frame. Following the refurbishment there's no library, no books and no mirror, and, from now on, when we want to change dimensions, we'll have to use the mirror in Andreu's bathroom. It will be rather unseemly if now and then we coincide with his midnight poos.

15 May

They are quite a grey couple and neither spends much time in the house. When he's not playing golf, Andreu is at the office in meetings, while Jacqueline goes to the gym, shops or is at her girlfriends'. If it weren't for the maid and the gardener, who shack up of an afternoon and offer us a few homespun porn sessions, it would be as tedious as ever here. Luckily, the couple watch TV in the evening.

25 May

It was a foregone conclusion that it would happen sooner or later. At midnight, when we were about to come out of Andreu's bathroom mirror, we caught him vomiting in the toilet bowl. As he was drunk and didn't get there in time, he left a fine mess. Tomorrow, Nati, the maid, will curse him to high heaven.

After Andreu came out of the bathroom, he and Jacqueline rowed because she didn't feel like doing it. She shut herself in their bedroom and he went down to the lounge in a rage. He almost fell and rolled down the staircase, but in the end collapsed on the sofa, switched on the telly and immediately fell asleep. We watched a porn film. To be honest, it was awful.

27 May

We're back in the little cupboard. Jacqueline says the house gives her bad vibrations and she's called Rafa again, who has burned more joss sticks, lit more candles and recited more exorcisms. I'd told Josep to watch it, that interfering in the dreams of the living creates problems, but he's as stubborn as a mule. He's been snooping in Jacqueline's dreams night after night and we're all paying for it now.

4 June

We've just come out of the cupboard and Rafa is back. On this occasion, however, he's not here to purify anything but to have a fling with the lady of the house, and they're both jiggling away in the bedroom right now. We've finally got a bit of action …!

Andreu is on a business trip, as Jacqueline told Rafa, who stayed overnight. In Jacqueline's favour, I should add that Andreu took his secretary with him, as well as some new underpants and a box of condoms. Personally, if I had to choose between Andreu and Rafa, I'd go for Andreu anytime. We all find Rafa and the gold chains he wears round his neck far too vulgar.

5 June

Elisenda smells a rat. She thinks Rafa is up to no good. As soon as she can she'll try to penetrate his dreams and see if she can find out what he's up to. But she will have to wait until midnight, because we can't do anything from this side of the mirror.

6 June

Elisenda is right: this guy is fishy. She didn't even have to enter his dreams to find out that he was plotting something. His own behaviour betrayed him.

As soon as Jacqueline fell asleep, Rafa got up silently and prowled round the house. He was looking for the safe, and when he found it hidden behind a painting, he grinned broadly. Old Andreu is so original. And interior designers too …!

The rascal also found the drawer where Jacqueline keeps her jewels, but he simply examined them one by one and put them back where they belonged. Then he rummaged in her handbag and took an imprint of the house keys. When they left the house mid-morning and Jacqueline switched on the alarm, he registered the combination and discreetly jotted it down on a piece of paper. Jacqueline is so stupid she didn't even notice. But one hardly needs to be Sherlock Holmes to know what Rafa is after.

11 June

Andreu is on another business trip and Rafa is back. We were all keen to go through the bathroom mirror at midnight and Elisenda entered his dreams. She emerged in a state of shock.

Rafa belongs to a gang of professional criminals who specialize in using esoteric nonsense to pull the wool over the eyes of the rich. They've not yet decided on a date, but now that they know the code for the alarm and where the safe and jewels are, they're intending to break in one night and force Andreu to give them the combination, because Jacqueline doesn't know what it is. They'll then shoot the two of them in cold blood so as not to leave any eyewitnesses.

12 June

Emergency meeting: we must act. If this guy and his gang do in Andreu and Jacqueline, they'll both turn into ghosts and stay on to live with us from now to eternity. We can't allow that, because Jacqueline and Andreu aren't family and, besides, they're deadly boring.

We organized a brainstorming session and everyone chipped in. Bernat suggested we terrorize Andreu and Jacqueline into abandoning the house, but that would risk Jacqueline summoning Rafa back with his joss sticks and we'd have to spend another week in the little cupboard.

The other proposals aren't even worth mentioning.

We are still pondering.

13 June

Still haven't come up with anything.

14 June

We're beginning to get nervous.

17 June

Antoni-intestines finally came up with a solution: we should scare the *thieves*, not the couple. When they open the door and walk into the house (let's hope they do so after midnight), we shall give them a little surprise that we hope won't be fatal, because I don't think any of us could stand being forced to share eternity with Rafa and his gold chains. Eugenia will be the first they'll see, mincemeat and head under arm, and then Anastase with his shattered face and nether regions. If they still haven't run off in fright, Antoni-intestines will come onstage. And if Antoni doesn't do the trick, the rest of us will enter wailing.

It's a fantastic strategy and we all congratulated Antoni. Let's hope we don't lose our nerve!

22 June

Yesterday was wonderful. At about four in the morning, Rafa turned up with his gang of three. Margarida, who was on guard duty, saw them come in and warned us straight away. As we had rehearsed it so often, our performance was perfect and the thieves legged it, terrified but alive. While Andreu rushed to ring the police,

Jacqueline recognized Rafa running across the garden like a madman. Luscious she may be, but she kept as quiet as a mouse. I don't think the police will catch them.

They soon came and changed the lock on the door, and Andreu has changed the combination on his safe as well as the alarm code. Jacqueline, who is still under sedation, has spent the whole day in bed.

Tonight, we're throwing a big party to celebrate.

We are the best!

15 July

Jacqueline and Andreu's lovemaking has considerably improved, particularly since she's putting more into it now. They still spend little time at home, but when they are here it's one interminable, cloying declaration of love. It makes some of us feel queasy.

The other novelty is that they have contracted a foreign butler who sleeps in the house and is licensed to carry weapons. He is a giant of a man and looks every inch a retired marine. According to Antoni-heart-attack, who has finally decided to come out of the closet, the butler is sexy, which explains why he and the maid are now humping.

The gardener suspects something and is beginning to feel riled. Ah, nothing like a good attack of jealousy to keep us entertained ...!

A spanner in the works. The gardener also has a pistol and is very angry. He has seen that they've locked the door on him and is wondering whether to dispatch the butler and the maid to the other side in true Spanish-jealous-lover style. Then he will shoot himself. Big-time melodrama. And, from our point of view, highly inconvenient.

Just in case the gardener's threats weren't merely hot air, we met last night and decided (though Antoni-heart attack was opposed to the plan) that we'd all pay the butler a polite visit tonight to see whether we can't scare the pants off him, so he disappears before something tragic happens. We have rehearsed our sequence.

Sorry, Paquita, but it would be the last straw if we were forced to cohabit eternally with the servants!

I'm a Vampire

I'm a vampire. One of the old guard. I can't even remember how long it's been. Nine hundred years, at the very least. But I have no complaints. Considering I'm a vampire, I'm in really good shape despite the centuries I've been around.

The vampire I once was and the one I am now share nothing in common. We are two different beings. I won't deny I've committed all kinds of excesses in the course of my lengthy career, but with time I've learned to curb my natural instincts. You could say I've become a very restrained vampire. It's true, circumstances didn't give me much choice. I've proved to be an adaptable beast.

When I first turned into a vampire, I did the usual: slept by day, went out by night and sucked the blood of virgins … Nowadays, ever since I discovered sunblock and can venture out whenever I feel like it, I'm more of a day person. I have greater freedom of movement, and that has helped me change my habits and enjoy new experiences; though, naturally, in the heat of high summer I don't act the fool; I stay put, prostrate in my crypt. Sun creams are all well and good; they cost the earth and leave grease everywhere, but a vampire without a single gram of melanin in his skin had better not take any risks. I've had a couple of upsets and don't want to end up being singed like a sausage.

I was born and became a vampire in Savall, a village that's now become an upmarket residential estate around a huge golf course. In the Middle Ages, when I was a youngster, Savall was a prosperous town, with a castle, a lord of the manor and a vampire. The lord of the manor and the vampire were one and the same, and the vassals were accustomed to the local feudal big shot – that is, yours truly – paying a night-time visit to suck the blood of their daughters. I still feel nostalgia for an era when virgins were reasonably easy to find and relations with the Church were good because the clergy were too busy burning heretics and expelling Jews, and left me to my own devices. What's more, a vampire in the locality was good for tourism: we pedigree, classy vampires were much in demand. The people of Savall couldn't complain: thanks to the gloomy air of my castle and the horrific stories they recounted about my misdeeds, the town was sitting on a regular gold mine.

The good folk of Savall soon accepted my nightly incursions and reacted phlegmatically. They never harassed me, and I in return sucked the blood of their daughters in moderation: very few died from my bites or were transformed into vampires. It's a hassle when you have more than one sleeping in the same crypt, and as I'd had a couple of bad experiences, I made sure I stopped biting the girls the second they showed the first signs of transmuting. On the other hand, the peasants always struggled to get together the money to pay the dowries for their daughters, and in years when there was a bad harvest or taxes were hiked, they felt relieved when I took the odd one to the other side. Some were so grateful they even sent me a card and a basket of hams and fruit for Christmas.

Unfortunately, things changed in Savall with the onset of the age of industrialization and all that nonsense about Marxism, atheism and the death of God. Psychoanalysis also did its best to downgrade me; it dubbed me a childhood trauma or worse, and the townspeople began to lose their respect for me. As some had read the novel by Bram Stoker (an Irishman, I ask you!), one fine day they decided to set fire to the castle and crypt, and they've been in a shocking state ever since: I'm not what you'd call a handyman. In any case, since the time the Fascists decided I was an anarchist because of my cloak (which sported the traditional red and black), I've always been very wary. The bastards executed me and threw me in a common grave, but as we vampires only die when someone thrusts a stake through our hearts or if we expose our skin to the glare of the sun, I immediately revived and flew back to the crypt. I hid there, drinking rats' blood and nibbling insects until the war ended. I survived the situation as best I could.

The fact is, I've become very refined over the centuries and have abandoned some unpopular practices. I've not sucked the blood of young girls for years, because I accept it's not the done thing any more. It's a barbaric custom. I survive by drinking the blood from the lambs and hens I keep in my yard, and, as all the small farmers have gone to live in the city after selling their land to the property developers, the Barcelona families who spend the summers and weekends here think I'm an eccentric and have invented a bunch of amusing anecdotes about me. That I run around stark naked when there's a full moon – as if we vampires had nothing better to do. That I'm a crazy artist who fetches high prices in New York (I really *should* do something with those tubes of sun cream piling up in the kitchen garden). Some reckon I'm a failed fashion designer, no doubt because I'm still wearing the same clothes I wore a couple of centuries ago, and others think that I'm an ecologist. The yard and kitchen garden I had built next to the crypt when the Germans bombed the castle and I was left homeless are indeed misleading. The shed and kitchen garden are for show, since I sleep in the crypt and my stomach can't cope with solids, but the yard and the animals are needed because I have to get my proteins from somewhere. All in all, my culinary habits aren't as peculiar as you might think. Or what the hell do people think goes into their *butifarra* sausages?

Until quite recently, then, my non-life as a vampire was a tranquil affair, and mostly hassle-free. Nevertheless, it all almost went pear-shaped a few months ago, when something happened that really upset me and which, to tell the truth, I still find perplexing.

*

It all began one particularly hot August afternoon. It was almost twilight, and I'd gone out to fly because the crypt was like an oven and nobody could have stood it in there. As the chemist's on the estate stays open till ten, I decided to pay a visit and buy a few tubes of sun cream. On my way to the shop in the centre of the sparse collection of houses that the spin merchants like to call a "village", I went down one of the avenues between the villas, which I like because the foliage of the plane trees is very thick and cool. While I was roaming, wondering what I should do next, I was surprised to see graffiti on the west-facing walls of one of the mansions and froze on the spot when I read it. Somebody had scrawled the word VAMPIRE in red paint.

I went around the house, scared stiff, and found a couple more bits of graffiti on the other garden wall. The first said SON OF A WHORE, and the second, YOU'RE A VAMPIRE, SORRIBES! My hair stood on end and I almost fainted. I could hardly believe my eyes: for the first time in many a century, a vampire from elsewhere had established himself in my territory (in fact, it's not really mine, but I like to pretend it is).

That unknown vampire and I had something in common – my mother had also earned an honest crust exercising the oldest trade in the world – but that was our only similarity. To begin with, this fellow lived in an upmarket mansion and not in a crypt where you could have baked bread at noon. Secondly, this Sorribes was a nomadic vampire, or at least a vampire who liked to travel, which was in itself intriguing, because everyone knows we vampires are territorial creatures and that, other than in exceptional circumstances, we don't like moving far, let alone going on holiday. We think that's very vulgar. Besides, as tradition forces us to sleep inside a coffin and directly above the land of our ancestors, travelling is real torture, not to mention the fact we end up paying a fortune in excess baggage. If this guy Sorribes decided to spend his cash this way, that was his choice, but I was worried by the fact that the people living on the Savall golf complex had flushed him out.

The presence of a self-styled vampire in the area could be a problem that would have an impact on me and my routine non-existence. I didn't know the habits of my colleague, and thus didn't know if he was a New Vampire or if he implanted his fangs and donned his cloak at twilight before flying off in search of a maiden's fresh blood. In any case, someone in Savall was clearly on the case. I decided to investigate, to be on the safe side.

As it was dinnertime and I was hungry, I forgot the sun cream and went back to the crypt and drank a lamb. While I was lying in my coffin digesting my meal, I thought up a strategy that would enable me to find out something without attracting too much attention or arousing the suspicions of my neighbours. I hadn't assumed the shape of a bat for years, but after carefully weighing up all the options I concluded that the best strategy would be to try to slip discreetly in through a window and take a look around. Right away. Thinking I'd take advantage of the fact it was night and that the vampire must have abandoned his nest, I donned my cloak and flew off in the direction of the villa.

I soon discovered I had a problem. Getting my bearings wasn't at all easy: there were too many aerials, satellite dishes and mobile phones sending out waves left, right and centre. We bats have very sensitive hearing, and my head soon felt like a football with all those waves bouncing around. After crashing into an electricity pole that knocked me out for a while, I decided to forget about flying and walk there like a normal person. As soon as I reached the mansion, I transformed myself back into a bat and started to look for a window so I could fly inside. After circling around and around, I was forced to accept that it was impossible to get in that way. The cunning bastard had air conditioning.

People used to sleep with their windows open in the summer, making it easy to creep in. New technology means that everyone sleeps with their windows shut when it's hot, so there's no way to get inside. Yet again defeated by the wonders of progress, I had to recover my human form and force an entry, a delicate operation that's never been one of my fortes. What's more, the mansion was full of alarms and security cameras, and finally I had to beat it before the police arrived. I clearly needed to try a different tactic.

The next morning, after I'd consulted my silk-lined pillow, I decided to speak to my friend Sebastià. Sebastià is a local Catalan policeman and we've known each other almost forever. As the residential estate has changed Savall into a desirable luxury golf complex and the wealthy are a bunch of paranoids, Sebastià drops by now and again on the pretext that he wants to see if I need anything and to check that all is in order. In fact, I know the summer holiday crowd think I'm rather offbeat and send Sebastià to keep tabs on me. That's fine as far as I'm concerned.

Sebastià is a fine fellow. He may not be very bright, but he's pleasant enough and full of common sense, a quality that's been lacking in these parts recently. He usually comes in his jeep once a week, about 9 a.m., and eats breakfast with me. When he finishes his filled roll and beer (he's theoretically on duty and isn't allowed to drink, but he knows I won't let on), we walk round the garden putting the world to rights. While he gossips, or complains that his wife spends too much with her credit card, I get him a bag of home-grown vegetables, which he says are very tasty because they're so obviously organic. He insists on paying, I refuse to take his money, though I finally relent. To tell the truth, if it weren't for Sebastià and his fondness for my vegetables, I don't how I'd afford my tubes of sun cream.

Thanks to our conversations, I know that he usually goes to Barbes's bar for a late-morning aperitif. Sebastià had already paid me his regular visit, so I decided to go and see him in the bar and try out my own skills as a detective.

They looked astounded when I walked in, because they know I never set foot in there. It's a place I avoid, basically because it annoys me that I can't drink alcohol and because Barbes has a huge mirror hanging over the counter and I'm afraid someone will notice I don't have a reflection. He also has a few strings of garlic hanging up next to the mirror, either to spice up his cooking or to add a rustic touch, but that's really not a problem, because all those stories they tell about vampires and garlic are pure supposition. It's true we're allergic to the sun, holy water and crosses, but garlic makes no odds. The only drawback is that if you sink a fang into the carotid artery of someone who's been eating aioli or a garlicky gazpacho it's really disgusting. The blood of garlic aficionados tastes awful and, what's more, makes you belch something awful.

I ordered vermouth and olives as routinely as possible and sat next to Sebastià, who was also surprised to see me. I justified my presence by saying I was on my way to the chemist's to buy painkillers because my back was hurting. We argued for a while about whether lumbago was more painful than kidney stones; the latter finally won out. Sebastià started talking about the water restrictions that locals were having to suffer because of the golf course, and the conversation immediately turned to the holiday crowd, their residential estate and the nuisance they caused. I easily steered it to what was concerning me and whether my friend knew anything about the new vampire who'd set up in town.

"Sebastià, what's the meaning of the graffiti on the wall of the villa next to the duck pond?" I asked, as deadpan as can be.

"Ah, yes … The Sorribes family!" Sebastià sighed. "A vampire's moved in, old boy!"

"You already know he's a vampire?"

"Of course! As soon as he bought the villa, we knew what he was. What gets me," Sebastià added, chewing an olive, "is that I now have to catch the idiots who painted the graffiti!"

"But if you know he's a vampire, why not simply kick him out?" I asked, even more perplexed.

"I'd like to, you bet …" he chuckled. But then he suddenly got all serious and shouted, "These sons of bitches have no right to suck our blood!"

"What's more, you've found him out. You know what he is. And thanks to the graffiti, everybody does."

"I tell you, forget the fucking graffiti!" Then, lowering his voice to a whisper, Sebastià leaned forward. "I'd personally string him up by his balls in the middle of the town square. That would teach him and his ilk a lesson!"

I nodded. I understood how Sebastià was feeling, because in my heyday I used to drive people crazy and stir up similar feelings. Anyway, I decided not to tell him it wasn't a good idea to string him up by the balls because he'd simply fly off.

"And is this fellow sucking your blood as well?" I'd heard of cases of vampires attacking sturdy, muscular men, but I'd always thought it must be a myth.

"Mine and the blood of everyone who's got a mortgage!" He sighed yet again. "And if only it were just him! But you're all right with your little house and garden. You're set for life!"

"Are you sure there's nothing you can do?" I insisted. "There must be a way to stop him in his tracks …"

Sebastià shrugged his shoulders and chewed another olive. "The Russians had a bash with their revolution, and look what happened! And the less said about Cuba the better."

So this Sorribes had wrought havoc in Russia and Cuba, and I was totally oblivious. That was only to be expected; I read *Cosmopolitan* rather than the broadsheets.

"Do you reckon his wife and children are vampires as well?" I asked, determined to leave the bar as well informed as possible.

"You bet!" Sebastià responded, apparently totally convinced. "You've only got to see his wife strutting around the golf club, as if she were a duchess … And their children are vile. If I told you what they get up to at night …"

"I think I can imagine …"

"Those kids will be worse than their parents, you mark my words," Sebastià concluded.

I conspicuously ate an olive and realized the whole bar was looking at us. I judged it sensible to change tack and talk about more mundane matters while pouring my vermouth on the sly into the pot with the rubber plant, which immediately perked up. When it came to the bill, Sebastià insisted on paying, and, as I'm always broke, I made a token protest but let him do the honours.

When we hit the road, that damned August sun was so blistering I had to rush back into the bar to avoid disintegrating. I used the excuse that my back was hurting, and Sebastià, who's a real ace, offered to drive me home in his jeep. Once I was home, I immediately went to the crypt to rest because I was smouldering all over. In the jeep I'd noticed my right hand had begun to smell scorched, so I took a painkiller before going to sleep. I also decided it was high time to install air conditioning in the crypt: I'm well aware it's most inelegant to be sleeping nude in the coffin.

I had nightmares all day. I was out of sorts. I was upset an unknown vampire was sucking my friend's blood, and decided I must do something. Killing vampires is no easy task, but I was clear that was what I had to do.

The first challenge would be breaking in by day and catching them all asleep. The second would be finding the stake for killing vampires; I'd no idea where I'd left it. I was forced to give the crypt a thorough clean, which took a couple of days because you can't imagine the junk that piles up over nine centuries. Finally, the stake surfaced in a corner next to the skeleton of my great-great-grandfather, covered in fungi and cobwebs. I cleaned it up and put it in a sports bag, next to the iron sword for decapitation. After transfixing vampires through the heart with a stake, you have the option of beheading them. There's been a lot of theoretical debate on the subject, but, as these vampires were from elsewhere and unfamiliar with our customs, I thought it better to err on the side of excess. When in doubt, go the whole hog. The sword was rusty and weighed a ton.

I chose a cloudy afternoon when it looked like rain to put my plan into action. I knew they had a maid, because Sebastià had told me, and also that she wasn't a vampire because the Sorribeses were sucking *her* blood too. I knocked on the door politely and the maid almost fainted. Sebastià and the other locals were used to my pallor (I'd explained it away one day by claiming that I'd used an anti-acne lotion as a teenager and had never recovered my dark skin), but people who have never seen me before are sometimes frightened by me. As the maid didn't seem to want to let me in, and looked as if she'd ring the police, I decided hypnosis was my only course of action.

I'd not hypnotized anyone for years. Initially it was an effort, because the girl was hysterical and unfocused, but I succeeded after a few seconds and was able to enter the villa. Hypnosis is supposedly one of the skills that we vampires enjoy, but some are more skilled than others. In my case it's not easy, as I've been cross-eyed since birth, but on this occasion my powers worked. Once I had the maid under control, I questioned her and she revealed that everyone except her, who had to do the ironing, took an afternoon nap. That was all I needed to know.

Stressed out at the idea of killing vampires, I started to look for the cellar, where I imagined the Sorribeses asleep in their coffins, but however much I searched, I couldn't find a door down to any crypt. I questioned the maid again and was shocked by what I learned.

The house didn't have a cellar and the family slept in bedrooms on the top floor. *O tempora! O mores!* Something totally unexpected! However, stranger things have been known. I took a deep breath and headed up the stairs, determined to carry out my plan. I opened the door of a very beguiling bedroom papered in a Laura Ashley floral pattern and immediately felt a shiver of pleasure run down my spine. The air conditioning was full on, and it was like an icebox inside despite the heat in the street. It was exactly the powerful piece of technology I needed in my crypt; I took a mental note of the brand and continued my inspection.

A middle-aged vampire was asleep in the bed, naked under a sheet: she gave me a real thrill. Rather reluctantly, I opened my bag and took out the stake and the sword. As I was surprised that she was sleeping in a bed and not in a coffin, I wanted to check she was one of us, so before starting on my task I lifted the sheet and touched her breast. She was indeed ice-cold. I stuck the stake through her heart before she could wake up, and then beheaded her. A deft, professional blow. Her head rolled across the floor, under the dressing table, and came to rest next to her slippers, which is where I left it spurting blood. I assumed the vampire must have had a feast before falling asleep, because the room was soon splattered in red and we vampires only bleed when digesting. The two youngsters were no problem either, but their room smelled pleasantly of strange herbs that put me on a high and made me want to laugh: while I was sticking the stake into Sorribes I did laugh, and the fool woke up. In fact, his screams rather dampened my spirits. Luckily, that was it.

The Sorribes vampires were history. Sebastià could stop worrying now. I retrieved my stake and sword and returned to my crypt, feeling as pleased as Punch at a job well done. The sight of so much blood had given me an appetite, and I decided to celebrate my feats with a couple of hens and a small lamb. As I was exhausted, I went off to rest in my comfortable coffin, wondering how I'd manage to slip in an electricity cable unnoticed and install air conditioning. That evening I dreamed of that lady vampire's breasts and at ten woke up with a hard-on.

The following morning Sebastià dropped by, and he didn't look too happy. I was still wearing the bloodstained shirt, but as Sebastià is red-green colour-blind, I decided to let it slide.

"What's new, Sebastià? Anything the matter?" I asked, knowing there'd been at least one change in town.

"For God's sake, haven't you heard about the disaster at the Sorribes mansion?" he replied, obviously distressed.

"No ..."

"Butchery, old boy! Real butchery! They've dispatched a contingent of police from Barcelona. The TV people are here as well! I've just popped by to tell you to watch out because there's a madman around."

"A madman?" I asked, taken aback.

"A very dangerous madman. Yesterday someone broke into the Sorribes villa and stabbed the lot of them. Chopped their heads off as well. The four of them: husband, wife and two kids. This morning the postman found the maid in a state of shock and discovered the corpses." He added in a worried voice, "This is a psychopath at work!"

"But he was a vampire …" I replied warily.

"Vampire or not, this was barbaric!" countered Sebastià indignantly.

"You said he was sucking your blood …"

"Yes … But they've been done in so brutally!" He went on, thinking aloud. "I expect it's one of those gangs from Eastern Europe …"

"I'm at a loss for words. You've chilled me to the bone. If you pricked me now, you'd not get a drop of blood out of me!"

"I know how you feel. In a case like this, you don't know what to say. Poor family! If you'd seen them …"

I was really confused. I thought Sebastià would be pleased I'd destroyed that colony of bloodsucking vampires, but that clearly wasn't the case. Something had gone wrong.

"Keep a watch out," he shouted as he left. "Keep your eyes peeled. And change that shirt, for Christ's sake. It's a mess!"

*

It's obvious I'm getting past it: there's no way I can understand these mortals. I've probably spent too long roaming this benighted world and the time has come to bid farewell. Basically, it's only fun being immortal if, in fact, you're not, and I've felt a little out of place for a couple of centuries amid so much modernity. What's the fun in being a vampire if people aren't frightened any more and the categorical imperative doesn't allow you to go around chomping on necks? What's the point in being immortal if you can't enjoy a bottle of Dom Pérignon or go to the Botafumeiro and have a proper shellfish blowout? These are the questions I've been asking myself of late, and I can find no answers. Perhaps the bottom line is that being a vampire isn't so wonderful. It's obvious I really got my wires crossed over the Sorribeses. I don't mean that Savall ought to organize a homage to me or name a street after me (though I don't see why not), but frankly I was expecting a different reaction. At the very least, I thought that Sebastià would be thrilled to bits.

At any rate, I did what a vampire had to do, and my conscience is clear. And isn't that what it's really all about? As my mother used to tell customers who couldn't get it up, at the end of the day, it's the thought that counts.

CONNECTIONS

A second note to readers:

Barcelona, the city where I was born and where I have lived for most of my life, is the setting for nearly all the stories in Connections. *And Barcelona is also the city to which all the characters belong, even in stories which are partly set in other areas of Catalonia. In this sense,* Connections *is a noirish mosaic that shows off different fragments of the city, its inhabitants and history. An ironic gaze drives most of these stories, built around one or two criminal acts with characters who generally don't belong to the city's underworld but live in the well-off or working-class neighbourhoods where violence goes hand in glove with intrigue and subterfuge.*

Although the stories in Connections *are independent, some characters and situations are related, whether obviously or obliquely. You must read carefully to identify the connections between one narrative and the others – and you don't have to read them in order to solve the puzzle. Reader, I am issuing you a challenge: spot the connections, the detail or character that makes each story a piece of this mosaic.*

Flesh-Coloured People

Hey now, I don't know if they were Chinese. You bet, they were Oriental, of course they were … But I'm not at all sure whether they were Chinese, Koreans, Vietnamese, Thai or Japanese. For fuck's sake, I didn't pay that much attention. I was shitting my pants at the sight of that pistol! In any case, it was my bad luck that thieves had decided to attack the place I'd gone to buy condoms. As if there weren't half a dozen other pharmacies in Sarrià …! And luckily I hadn't got around to asking for the condoms, so when Daddy asked me what I was doing in that particular pharmacy (it wasn't where we usually go to buy our medicines), I was able to cover up by saying I needed some ibuprofen because my period was due and I'd got stomach cramps. (Daddy likes to think he's cool, but when he hears the word "period" he goes all funny.)

It really was a stroke of luck that they called Daddy, because if it had been Mummy she would have remembered my period was a week away and given me the third degree. And not because buying condoms is a problem – quite the contrary, though I'm shy of mentioning the subject to Daddy, and poor Mummy is such a bore. To start with, she'd have congratulated me for being *such* a responsible young woman (well, we've been talking about them ever since I was *twelve!*), and you bet she'd have taken the opportunity to lecture me about not letting any boy bully or mistreat me, that I mustn't do anything I don't want to, etc. etc. Fuck, as if I was going to let any bastard lay his hands on me or tell me who I can go out with or what I should wear! What the hell does she think? That because I'm sixteen I don't have a mind of my own? And, wait for it, then she'd have segued to the boyfriend question and wanted to know what I was intending to do with the condoms (as if that wasn't obvious) and we'd have been at it all day. And, quite frankly, I don't want to tell her I fancy Biel and was planning how I'd lay him tonight after the Beyoncé concert. (You talk about this kind of thing with your mates, not with your mother, for heaven's sake. Why doesn't she *ever* get that?)

In any case, after what happened in the pharmacy, I might as well forget the concert. Shit, after all the effort it took to squeeze the cash out of the parents for my ticket, and now it looks like I won't be able to go … Why can't the *mossos* wait until tomorrow to take a statement and show me the photos? But obviously, as I wasn't injured and they say I'm psychologically unharmed, they asked Daddy's permission to take me to the police station … and who knows when we'll finish! The pharmacist was lucky; she was so hysterical the ambulance guys gave her a pill to calm her down and in the end sent her home. I reckon at the very least she'd had an anxiety attack, because the poor dear couldn't stop crying and shaking ... On the other hand, yours truly didn't shed a tear, even though I'm the kind that sobs her heart out at any romantic, *Titanic* kind of film. Who'd have thought it! One of the policewomen noticed how I was upset because I hadn't cried, and told me not to worry, that if I didn't react it didn't mean I was an unfeeling psychopath (well, she didn't exactly say that, but I understood what she was hinting at), but that I was simply still in a state of shock. Hell, you're not kidding! I'd never been held up at gunpoint before or seen anyone die (in real life, that is), let alone like that. Bang-bang, a couple of shots and you're on your way to the other side. You'll soon see when I put the photos on Instagram that I took before the police arrived (of the dead man, I mean, not the thieves). Oh, now I really regret not daring to take a selfie ... (I don't suppose it's a crime to put photos of a dead man out there?) Or perhaps it is? Anyway, I'd better ask around. I don't want to get into some other pile of shit.

The policeman who's busy showing me photos of criminals from their files tries to act nice and offers me a Coca-Cola. Will it look bad if I take out my mobile and take a quick peek? What with one thing and another, I've not checked my messages for some time, and, besides, I really ought to tell Claudia and Martina that most likely I won't be able to go to the concert because a guy's been killed at a chemist's and now I'm in a police station trying to identify the thieves. I reckon it's a waste of time and that the *mossos* shouldn't have any high hopes because it all happened so quickly and I registered fuck all. When I saw that they were about to shoot that guy, my legs caved and I shut my eyes; I was sure they'd do me and the chemist in so as not to leave any witnesses. That makes sense, doesn't it? As you see, despite all my worst fears, the thieves didn't kill us. After shooting, they turned tail and not only didn't take any drugs from the shelves, but didn't even look to see if there was cash in the till. I don't get it. The poor fellow they shot didn't even open his mouth! He looked like a foreigner (I'd say he was English, because I heard the "Oh my God!" he let out when he fell to the ground), but he didn't try to act the hero or anything like that. In fact, the thieves started shooting at him before they asked us for our money, as if they'd only come for him. Who knows, perhaps they got scared. But it all seems very strange, I mean the fact that they didn't steal anything from the pharmacy and spared our lives. Don't those guys watch any films or TV or anything? Everyone knows that when you charge into a shop to commit a robbery, you cover your faces so eyewitnesses can't identify you, especially if you shoot one of them. (If the bastards had thought to wear masks, I wouldn't be here now looking at photos and would still have time to go home and change and get to the concert on time.)

Obviously, if it depends on me, the *mossos* will be hard-pressed to identify those killers. OK, so I *am* Chinese and was born in Beijing, but, you know, all Chinese look the same to me. As I was brought up in Sarrià, the only Orientals I'm used to seeing (apart from tourists) are the ones who run the bazaar near my secondary school, the one that used to be called the One-Euro Shop, and the family that now runs Manel's bar (I'm not sure whether they are Chinese or Korean). What I'm saying is that I may look as Oriental as you like, but my name is Eulàlia Gasull i Balasch and I've lived here almost all my life – in other words, the fact that the criminals and I belong to the same race is no help at all in this case. (Come to think of it, Mummy told me it's racist to talk about "race". Hell, what did she tell me you ought to say? Ethnics? Ethnic group? I don't remember.) Besides, I didn't understand a single word they said; however Chinese I might look, I don't understand any Chinese. I don't even know how to say "hello", even though, a couple of years ago, on the pretext that I was born in China, Mummy insisted I should learn Mandarin and signed up a private tutor (who, by the way, wasn't Chinese but one of her colleagues at uni). Good God, what a complicated language it is! I lasted a couple of weeks (though my teacher was brilliant), and that was only to keep up appearances. The fact is, I prefer sciences and have enough on my plate trying to pick up a smattering of English to want to bother tackling a language as fiendishly difficult as Mandarin.

I may have been born in China, but I have nothing in common with China. But you try telling Mummy that. I don't even have Chinese friends. Not a single one. And not because I've anything against them, right? As I said, at the end of the day the Chinese or Orientals I have bumped into and know by sight (like the ones in the shop or the bar) aren't my age and aren't chatty either. All my friends (both boys and girls) are locals (I mean they're not adopted), so I'm not used to seeing Oriental faces. It's hardly my fault if I can't distinguish one Oriental from another, now, is it? Hell, they all look the same to me! I'm not sure, perhaps if my parents had sent me to a state school it would have been easier for me to relate to people of my race (or ethnic group), but they decided to send me to a Catalan progressive school where the only foreigners were a half-Dutch girl who wasn't even in my class and a Scottish boy who was incredibly freckled and ginger-haired. There were no Chinese (or Korean, Vietnamese, etc.) pupils; I don't know whether that was because the school was too expensive or because hardly any Orientals lived in Sarrià.

If the *mossos* are expecting me to identify the attackers because I happen to be from an Oriental race (or ethnic group), they'll be in for a long wait. And it's lucky that Mummy won't be back until later tonight (she works at the uni and had to go to Madrid today as an external examiner) because, knowing her, she'd already have blasted the police, accusing them of being racist and a lot more besides. And, frankly, the last thing I need right now is one of Mummy's little tantrums. She's no joke when she gets wound up. And it doesn't take much. You know, it's not that I don't agree that there are racists galore, but she's got her radar on full all the time, and doesn't miss a single opportunity. Fuck, you'd think she belonged to the far left … She's so bloody politically correct that, when she's around, everybody has to watch out they don't put a foot wrong, and even then she'll find something to grouse about. And it's not as if Daddy and me don't tell her to give us a break, that there's no need to be on our case all the time. Not long ago she hit the roof because she heard me say I'd been to eat at a Jap with my girlfriends. A Jap! You know, we don't mean anything wrong by that (in fact, if we were racist, we wouldn't go to eat in their restaurants now, would we?). Not to mention the Pakis, another word that's banned at home because Mummy says it shows contempt. What are we supposed to call the Pakis, given that "Pakistanis" is such a long word to use that nobody bothers? She even reckons it's racist to say flesh is flesh-coloured, for Christ's sake! She says you should say "beige", because flesh can be many colours (for example, she says black people aren't "flesh-coloured"). Well, maybe she's right in this case, but I reckon it's treading a fine line … Besides, beige is brown rather than flesh-white, I reckon. And, according to the dictionary (I consulted one once, out of curiosity), beige is a "yellowy grey", while everyone knows that flesh-coloured means a light brownish pink. If I've ever had to paint something flesh-coloured, I knew what it meant: you take a light brown and add a touch of pink. (If you take grey and add yellow, you don't get "flesh-coloured", you get the colour of summer diarrhoea.)

It's like the mania she's got for China. Fuck, if she likes China so much, why doesn't she go there by herself? She's decided we must go whether we like it or not, so this summer, instead of going to Cadaqués as we do every year, we're going to spend August tramping around China on one of those package deals that only rich pensioners or couples who spend the whole time with their tongues down each other's throats go on. And not just two or three weeks, but the whole damned month! You can imagine how thrilled I am! Especially since this year Claudia and Martina and I were intending to go to Ibiza for a week and we'd planned every detail. Where we would sleep (on the beach, to save money, though we weren't going to tell our parents that), the discos we'd go to, the clothes we'd take … Right, if Mummy wants to have *family* holidays, as she puts it, she might have listened to me a *teeny* bit and organized a trip to the States, for example, as that's somewhere I'm keen to visit. I'd even sketched out a route that went via New York, San Francisco and Los Angeles and included a visit to an Indian reservation (I'm sure you shouldn't say that, but, for heaven's sake …), thinking that would convince her … But no chance. We must go to China, she says, so I can be in touch with my *origins*. As if at this point in my life I give a shit about all that … Sure, I know she's doing this with the best of intentions, and I'm not saying that later on, when I'm older, I won't want to know more about the country where I was born and all that jazz … But hell, right now I couldn't care less about China! How should I put that to her? In Chinese? I'm even allergic to MSG and don't like Chinese food ...! I've got other priorities right now, and, to be honest, I must say that I'm not all that keen on the Chinese. Yes, I know that doesn't sound very nice (God help me if Mummy heard me say that), but it's out of my hands. I mean, those guys (that is, my biological parents) left me in a basket on the steps of an orphanage knowing full well how lousy those institutions are in China. And if they already had a son and couldn't have any more, given that the law ruled that out, as Mummy says, they could have fucking well used a condom, right? Or were condoms banned in China at the time? Give me a break ...

The policeman says I look as if my mind is on other things and that I should concentrate. But how on earth can I concentrate if all the faces look the same? All I can think about is that it's only two hours till the concert and I'm wasting my time here. Fucking hell, why do I always have to be so unlucky? Of course, I don't want to seem insensitive, I know a human being has died, etc., but what about me? This Biel business is more complicated than you'd think, and it wasn't easy setting it up so I could go to see Beyoncé and go home with him afterwards. And he's so good-looking! Fair hair, green eyes and tanned skin (his parents own a yacht in the port of Llavaneres and he's got that seaside dark tone that's a bit like the colour of Beyoncé's skin, not flesh-flesh but nor would you call it black-black; caramel, more like). And, by the way, I'm quite a looker too. Maybe my tits let me down – they're on the small side – but unlike Claudia (who's always on a diet, poor thing), I'm svelte, clothes always look good on me and I can wear leggings with short, tight-fitting tops that don't ever reveal any bulges. I'd bought the prettiest black T-shirt for the concert, the kind that shows off your navel, with a plunging neckline and sequinned straps. The advantage of having small tits is that I don't need to wear a bra and can make my nipples stick out; at least one thing compensates for the other. Not at school, where they've hauled me up a couple of times on account of my nipples being on display, which I think is quite unfair. I mean, what about the girls who've got big tits? Don't the guys' eyes swallow them whole? Like Neus, who wears the tightest jerseys in summer and the teachers never say a word. And you watch how she'll come on to Biel tonight if I'm not there! Knowing Biel, he'll go along with her, because Neus *is* pretty and she knows how to hook a guy. What a pile of shit this is!

And, for Christ's sake, these fellows look so evil! Their faces say it all! I don't know, perhaps I should pick out a couple and wind this farce up for good. After all, you bet they're guilty of something, otherwise the police wouldn't have them on file. Besides, the *mossos* will investigate whether they really are the men who tried to hold up the pharmacy, won't they? Because what's going to happen to them? They'll only arrest them for a few hours, while they check out their alibis. And if I have any regrets, I can always return to the station and retract what I said. I was in a state of shock and confused, I'd not had anything to eat and my sugar count was low … You know, the typical excuses people make in these situations. If we leave now, and I can persuade Daddy to drive me, I can still get to the Palau Sant Jordi before the concert starts. I don't think I've got time to go home and change my clothes. Or shave my legs, but I can always do that on the sly in Claudia's bathroom if in the end Biel and I get together (Claudia's parents are away and we were intending to sleep at her place). The trousers and T-shirt I'm wearing are pretty tatty, that's true (the trousers have got the odd bloodstain at the bottom, although you'd hardly notice), but that would be better than missing the concert. What a drag! The outfit I'd selected for tonight was such a good fit …

Now I just have to decide which of these fellows will pick up the tab for what happened at the chemist's. Ugh, who should I choose? They've all got criminal mugs … And not because they are Orientals, but you tell me if they don't look as if they've just done their grandmother in … Obviously it's quite a big deal to accuse someone like this. Because what if I'm to blame for them putting someone inside the slammer who turns out to be innocent? You know, the remorse might go to my head and do my brain in. These things do happen … Fuck, I don't know what I should do … Perhaps I should stop playing games and tell the police the truth. And confess that, even though I might have Chinese *origins*, I'm totally unable to tell one Oriental from another and that all this is one big waste of time. And I need to leave right now, because I've got tickets for the Beyoncé concert and I'd like to go home, change my clothes and make myself up a bit …

Though I'm feeling quite exhausted, as if I'd run the marathon. I don't know what's coming over me all of a sudden … I reckon I'm going to spew up and I feel dodgy. That's all I needed, I don't know what's wrong … Now I really do feel like a good cry. And what about these flashes … And the whistling in my ears and that …

The Second Mrs Appleton

There wasn't a day in the last eighteen months when Mr Appleton hadn't rued divorcing the first Mrs Appleton in order to marry the second Mrs Appleton, who rejoiced in the first name of Paige. Mr Appleton was a career diplomat and had met his second wife in the offices of the British Embassy in Rome when he was the ambassador and she had been a part-time, low-level temp. Mr Appleton was fifty-six when he made the acquaintance of the second Mrs Appleton, who was twenty-five.

Mr Appleton was born in Woodstock, a small town located next to Blenheim Palace, the country residence of the Duke of Marlborough, and privileged to be one of the cohort of distant relatives of the first duke of the tribe – the famous "Marlborough's gone to war" – and the illustrious Winston Churchill. He had been a contemporary of Violet, the first Mrs Appleton, at Oxford where they were both students, and had married her shortly before taking up what was to be his first diplomatic posting abroad and packing their cases to go to Kampala.

Mr Appleton had come to the embassy in Rome thirty years after beginning that life as a vagabond bureaucrat in the capital of Uganda, heralded by a vaunted series of successes and a marriage that had lasted thirty years and given him two children. Little did Mr Appleton imagine his life would be turned upside down in the Italian capital, that he'd divorce and remarry, let alone that he'd soon be regretting replacing the competent, discreet first Mrs Appleton with the young, scatty Paige.

As he was a man of austere character and rigid persuasions, Mr Appleton disapproved of extramarital entanglements, which he criticized in private. Nevertheless, the arrival on the scene in Rome of the second Mrs Appleton caught him at a moment in his life when the past seemed to stretch out like a piece of chewing gum and the future was shortening like the days of winter, and he decided to make an exception. He liked the exception so much that what was meant simply as a weekend fling – a weekend when the first Mrs Appleton was visiting their children in London – finally turned into a torrid affair that would lead him back to the altar.

The second Mrs Appleton liked to tell people it had been love at first sight, and though *he* wasn't so happy to recall the memory – the moment the spark ignited, he had still been married to the first Mrs Appleton, and their audience would compare dates – the fact was that Mr Appleton had suffered a *coup de foudre* in the Italian capital and had been knocked for six.

The lack of an attractive physique wasn't among the second Mrs Appleton's defects, and that was a decisive factor in triggering their affair. The second Mrs Appleton was a freckled Englishwoman with wild, blonde hair, a green-eyed lioness with a come-on smile and moist lips and the necessary curves and bra size to make headway in life without needing to nurture any other talents. Mr Appleton's sex life, it has to be said, had never been characterized by fireworks, but the first Mrs Appleton's encounter with the menopause had reduced it to the category of a damp squib he was hard pressed to ignite half a dozen times a year. Unlike Violet, the second Mrs Appleton possessed all the splendour of the best pyrotechnics on New Year's Eve, and the diplomat was so dazzled by her exhibition of rockets, bangers, Bengal candles, crackers, yellow rain and multicoloured fountains that, when the first Mrs Appleton returned from London, he quickly gave her a new credit card and sent her to holiday by herself in New York.

For a couple of weeks while the first Mrs Appleton went to concerts and emptied the shops in Manhattan, Mr Appleton and the second Mrs Appleton had a ball filling embassy annexes and Rome's hotels with a fug of pheromones. However, the second Mrs Appleton, unwilling to play a secondary role in that *ménage à trois*, wasn't slow in confronting Mr Appleton with the dilemma of whether to transform the first Mrs Appleton into an ex-Mrs Appleton or to return to a diet of damp squibs. Overwhelmed by a second rush of adolescence to his groin that only lacked a spate of acne, Mr Appleton didn't think twice: he asked Violet for a divorce and regaled the future second Mrs Appleton with a diamond and emerald ring to put a seal on their betrothal.

Shortly after marrying the second Mrs Appleton in a discreet ceremony in Rome, Mr Appleton was appointed ambassador to Washington and the couple began experiencing problems. The second Mrs Appleton had always looked forward to living in the United States, but her enthusiasm soon waned when she discovered that Washington wasn't as entertaining as Rome and Americans weren't as dishy as Italians. Unlike the first Mrs Appleton, the second Mrs Appleton wasn't used to the slavish restrictions of protocol and soon tired of performing like a dummy at banquets and interminable receptions. Her ignorance of any area of knowledge that wasn't covered by the glossies made her stick out like a sore thumb, and forced her to remain silent most of the time: she was bored stiff. Tedium led her to chase the waiters and seek refuge in champagne, and champagne liberated her tongue and encouraged her to say the first thing that entered her head.

The first Mrs Appleton had set very high standards, and Mr Appleton began to make comparisons. The first Mrs Appleton had a degree in French literature, was the cousin twice removed of the queen's second cousin and had completely mastered the art of etiquette. In the case of the second Mrs Appleton, she had a degree in interior design from Buckinghamshire New University – a university that at the time enjoyed the dubious honour of hovering near the bottom of the British universities league table – and lacked the pedigree that equips one's DNA with the ability to match flowers, tablecloths and cutlery. And, above all, she was unable to keep her mouth shut. If the first Mrs Appleton knew when to be quiet without Mr Appleton having to give her a wink or kick her under the table, the second Mrs Appleton was an expert at putting her foot in it at the most inglorious of moments.

Mr Appleton soon had to spend more time keeping an eye on his wife than on international politics. However, that didn't curtail the second Mrs Appleton's indiscretions or prevent the provocative dresses she wore – she'd begun to shorten the length of her skirts and lower her necklines dangerously – from becoming a matter of gossip in Washington, and the jokes about the ambassador's ever-so-young wife's lack of know-how soon crossed the pond and came to the attention of Downing Street. Realizing the risks his brand-new wife's inexperience was exposing him to, Mr Appleton began to long for the professional savoir-faire of his first wife and to regret divorcing her.

Rock bottom was reached when they'd been in Washington for six months and the minister in charge asked him to organize a banquet to conclude a summit. Mr Appleton saw this as a test of his ability to represent Great Britain in the United States, and was conscious of what was at stake. He decided to take the bull by the horns and leave the second Mrs Appleton at the periphery of all the preparations.

With the subtlety that was the stock-in-trade of the profession he had chosen, Mr Appleton asked the second Mrs Appleton to offer her apologies on the day of the gala on the excuse that she had flu, and she readily agreed. However, she soon regretted acquiescing so meekly to her husband's peculiar request, and on the day of the dinner she had second thoughts and asked the waiters to add another place to the top table. What sense did it make, she told herself, for Mr Appleton to have such a young, pretty, amusing wife and keep her under wraps?

While he was waiting for his guests to arrive at the embassy, Mr Appleton had to suppress a panic attack when he saw his wife slink into the reception room, where the aperitifs were being served, in a figure-hugging black satin dress that left little to the imagination. Intimidated by the sight of so many heads of state and stuck-up first ladies, the second Mrs Appleton managed to remain reasonably sober until the desserts, when the appearance of bottles of bubbly meant the lack of inhibition she had begun to feel with the cocktails transformed into out-and-out euphoria and she felt the need to share her extravagant excesses with all the other guests.

The less than appropriate comments made by the second Mrs Appleton on delicate issues of international politics led to Mr Appleton's immediate dismissal the morning after and he was forced to return to London, where he had to choose between a small, windowless office in a Whitehall basement or early retirement. However, Mr Appleton still had friends in the British capital, and after knocking on lots of doors and recalling old favours, he managed a posting to Barcelona as a replacement for the outgoing consul. Everybody knew that to move from ambassador to consul was to plummet down the diplomatic ladder, but Mr Appleton explained it away by saying it was a personal favour he was doing the Prime Minister, who required someone she could trust in the Catalan capital to keep her informed about the manoeuvres of the independence-bound government and the strategies of the opposition.

The second Mrs Appleton was delighted by the idea of going to Barcelona. She'd never been there, but she had seen Woody Allen's film and been bowled over by the colourful portrait the film-maker had painted of the city. The prospect of hobnobbing with toreros and bohemian artists and spending the day on the beach quaffing sangria translated into a temporary resurgence of her amatory habits that had recently gone into hibernation. Infected by his wife's youthful ardour, Mr Appleton decided to give their marriage a second chance, trusting that Paige had learned her lesson.

Nonetheless, what promised to be a second honeymoon on the Med was short-lived. From the moment she arrived in Barcelona, the second Mrs Appleton busied herself redecorating the house they'd rented in Sarrià and shopping on the Passeig de Gràcia. She didn't bother to read the memorandum they'd sent her from London and, inadvertently, during the ceremony to accredit the new consul at the Palau de la Generalitat, she put her foot in it yet again. She wondered out loud why the hell the Catalans had to speak Catalan if they could already speak Spanish, which didn't go down at all well, and a shamefaced Mr Appleton had to humiliate himself and offer all manner of apologies to avoid the autonomous government's protests reaching the formal complaint stage and the Foreign Office in London. In the end, there was no such fallout, but Mr Appleton saw that the thread supporting the sword of Damocles hanging over his career was fraying by the second.

The second Mrs Appleton was one big disappointment. And not simply because her lack of brainpower had destroyed his ambition to retire from his career in the most important embassy on the planet, but also because the antidepressants and tranquillizers she'd started taking in order to survive the boredom of diplomatic life had transformed the revitalized fireworks of their sex life into a low-budget backstreet fling. Aware that that jamboree, like his career, was in implacable decline, he started to weigh up the idea of divorcing the second Mrs Appleton and trying to get back together with his ex.

However, Mr Appleton soon discovered that disentangling himself from the second Mrs Appleton was going to be far from easy. His present consort wasn't as docile as his first had been, and, when he insinuated that perhaps the moment had come to end a relationship that was foundering rather than developing, the second Mrs Appleton reacted by rejecting the option of divorce and threatening to mount a scandal of epic proportions with a kiss-and-tell interview in the *Sun* if he sent a lawyer her way.

That was the day Mr Appleton sidelined the divorce option and seriously began to contemplate the possibility of becoming a widower.

With the meticulous attention to detail that had been a feature of his life, Mr Appleton began to assess the various alternatives on offer if he were to rid himself of the second Mrs Appleton via the convenient method of dispatching her to the other side. He felt that suicide was the least risky option, and, making the most of a note in his possession that could be read as a goodbye message, he wasted no time in activating the plan that had occurred to him.

In no uncertain terms, Mr Appleton had forbidden the second Mrs Appleton from sending photos or messages by phone (he was afraid she'd hit the wrong button and send her documents to the wrong person's inbox), and as a result she had become accustomed to leaving him short notes on the pillow or bedside table when she felt a need to apologize after she'd embarrassed him. Mr Appleton quickly read these notes and threw them in the wastepaper bin (her spelling mistakes really grated on him), but, luckily, he had kept one she had written to him in Washington immediately after the reception where she had ruined his career. The handwritten note said "I'm so sorry, love" and was signed off with her first name. The only drawback was that, below her signature, the second Mrs Appleton had drawn an erect penis and two hairy testicles, which she had enhanced with a sensual kiss from her red lips. It didn't look like your average suicide note, but as everyone in Barcelona was becoming familiar with the second Mrs Appleton's wayward character and aversion to formalities, Mr Appleton thought it would pass muster and decided to go for it.

Mr Appleton chose a Saturday early in September when their maid was on holiday to terminate his wife's life. It was the day he had offered to accompany a member of the English Parliament to see a performance of *The Twilight of the Gods* at the Liceu opera house. The second Mrs Appleton hated opera, and, knowing his wife's tastes, Mr Appleton assumed she would refuse to swallow four and a half hours of Wagner just for the sake of appearances.

"Don't you worry, it's only a Labour MP. No need for you to suffer," Mr Appleton told her, laughing it off.

The performance began at seven. At about four, when the second Mrs Appleton was curled up on the sofa zapping through the channels, Mr Appleton took a bottle of cava from the fridge, opened it and slipped in a handful of tranquillizers he had previously rendered into powder with the help of a spoon. Then he walked into their dining room and, like a real gentleman, offered his wife a glass of cava knowing she wouldn't be able to resist the temptation of a drop of bubbly. Moved by his gesture, the second Mrs Appleton thanked him for thinking of her and went on to knock back the whole bottle.

She immediately fell asleep. Mr Appleton helped her to their bedroom on the second floor of their house, but rather than leaving her on top of the bed, he dragged her into the en suite bathroom, stripped her and lifted her into the bath. While the bath was filling up with hot water, Mr Appleton fetched a knife from the kitchen, returned to the bathroom and slit her wrists.

When the second Mrs Appleton was knocking on the gates of St Peter, Mr Appleton grabbed the bottle of cava, the glass and the note he was intending to use as a suicide missive, and took the lot into the bathroom. He slowly removed his fingerprints from places where they shouldn't be, checked that everything was in order and finally changed his clothes, combed his hair, sprayed scent over himself and went to the garage to get his car.

It was hot and muggy outside. As Mr Appleton drove out of his garage, he didn't notice the two men following close behind in a grey Ford Focus that had been parked outside his house for a couple of days. He had agreed to meet the Labour MP at 6.30 in the foyer of the Liceu and didn't want to arrive late, but the glass of cava (from a different bottle) that he had been obliged to drink in order not to arouse suspicion was making him feel queasy and headachy. As the opera they were about to see was on the long side, he decided to stop at a pharmacy to buy anti-acid tablets and painkillers. He found one open on the Carrer Escoles Pies, double-parked his car and went inside.

The only people in the shop were an adolescent girl rummaging on a shelf and the chemist. Mr Appleton strode towards the counter, not noticing the two men come in who had followed him from his house and into the pharmacy. The second he heard male voices speaking threateningly in a language that sounded like Chinese and saw the expression of panic on the shop assistant's face, he swivelled around and found himself facing two Oriental-looking men and one pistol aimed at himself.

Two shots rang out.

Mr Appleton fell to the floor, mortally wounded. And while his life ebbed away, he remembered the fragment of a conversation he had overheard in the course of one of those acts of protocol he'd had to attend, and how the now deceased second Mrs Appleton's ears had pricked up when a jaded inspector of the *mossos d'esquadra* had mentioned the new fashion for contracting Chinese hitmen through the pages of *The Times*.

Paradise Gained

Sergi couldn't think how to tell his girlfriend he wasn't going to be able to go on holiday. It was no use saying he was broke – Marisol knew he worked for his uncle and that he paid him a decent wage – or that work was preventing him from taking a fortnight off to get a tan on a beach with a backdrop that was rather more picturesque than the three cement chimneys of the old Sant Adrià de Besòs power station. Even Senyor Benito, Sergi's uncle, had shut up shop and taken his wife to his village to get away from the muggy heatwave. And Marisol, who'd been waiting for weeks to show off the silvery bikini she'd bought in the sales, began to lose patience.

"I don't get it, Sergi. There are some really great bargains on offer! And it's stifling in Barcelona ..."

Marisol lived in Gràcia in a flat-share with various friends from the faculty, psychology students like herself, and Sergi in Sant Adrià. They'd been going out for a couple of years, and were now at a stage in their relationship when they were starting to make plans to live together the moment Marisol finished her Masters in Clinical

Psychology and got a job. Sergi was a musician – he played the sax – but, as he couldn't live by music alone, he was forced to work for his uncle while he tried to build up a reputation by performing in bars and festivals with the jazz quartet he had set up with friends.

What Marisol didn't know (Sergi hadn't told her) was that her boyfriend was the favourite nephew of Senyor Benito, one of the old gangsters from the neighbourhood of La Mina. Experience had taught Sergi that going on about the criminal nature of the family business usually provoked a hostile reaction, and that's why he'd told Marisol what he told everyone who wasn't part of that delinquent scenario of intrigue on seedy side streets, in warehouses on the city's outskirts or down-at-heel bars: he'd say his uncle had a transport company that did house removals and haulage, and that he worked occasionally for him as a driver.

The circumstances that were stopping Sergi from going on holiday went back to a casual conversation Senyor Benito had had with the lawyer who looked after his clan's legal disputes. Sergi's uncle had complained that a disadvantage of his business was the extraordinary amount of cash it generated that he couldn't put in the bank, that he was forced to lodge bundles of notes in different hiding places, which was always stressful, because Sant Adrià was now full of gangs that did their own thing and didn't kowtow to him. His lawyer, who thanks to the fees he earned from the frequent visits Senyor Benito's employees made to Can Brians prison lived better than the Corleones' *consigliere*, told him that the best way to avoid such headaches would be to open an account in a tax-free paradise, which was what most of his customers had done.

"You don't even have to take a plane, because it's all done anonymously by computer. In fact, if you're interested, my brother-in-law would do it for a commission," his lawyer said.

"If it's so easy, why don't *you* do it and pocket the commission?" retorted Senyor Benito, who never trusted lawyers when it came to money, least of all his own.

"You know, it's easy enough, but you need to be up to speed with the internet and know how to navigate the dark web."

"The what?"

"The dark web, the part of the internet that's home to hackers."

"Oh …"

That day, at the entrance to the courthouse, Senyor Benito told his lawyer he'd think about it, simply to put him off. He thought the idea was interesting, but, as he was suspicious by nature and didn't want to depend on third parties who might take advantage of his ignorance to bamboozle him, he decided to bypass his lawyer and suggest to his sparkiest nephew that he ought to study computers with the aim of opening an offshore account for him.

Sergi was twenty-four and reputed to be smart. His father, one of Senyor Benito's brothers, had died at the end of the nineties during one of those gang wars that contribute to the improvement of the species via the natural selection of weapons chosen to liquidate all rivals. From a young age, Sergi had needed to be a live wire when it came to earning his keep, and Senyor Benito soon saw that the future of his youngest nephew didn't reside in his (non-existent) biceps or in his (scant) skills when it came to intimidating bad payers, driving second-hand Transit vans at top speed or using a knife without getting hurt, but in his ability to use his brain when it came to making decisions.

"So, Uncle, why exactly do you want me to study computers?" asked Sergi the day the patriarch suggested he should go back to reading books.

Senyor Benito prided himself on being a wily old bird, and preferred not to tell his nephew what he had in mind.

"Oh, you know, these computers are beyond me. But I can't rely on Paco and Manel, as you well know. They may be my sons, but they don't have your brains."

"And in the meantime, what am I going to live on? Because if I'm going to be studying, I won't be able to make any more deliveries ..." Sergi replied, fishing.

"Don't you worry, I'll still pay you a monthly wage. You just make sure you get top marks, right?"

Sergi, unlike his relatives, didn't have criminality in his blood and hated chasing around with his crazy cousins; he thought he'd won the lottery, and rushed to tell Marisol the good news. As the world of education was a remote, unknown galaxy for Senyor Benito, Sergi opted for a nine-month computer course in a backstreet academy in Badalona.

But Sergi soon discovered that he was even less interested in computers than in being a gangster, and stopped going to his classes. He was bored, and as he knew it was easy to hoodwink his uncle, who could barely switch on a computer, he decided to forget the academy and invest his monthly income in a giant TV, loudspeakers and a brand-new sax.

They were the happiest times of his life. Sergi pretended to go to his classes, and when his uncle asked him if he was learning a lot, he assured him that starting to study computers was the best decision he'd ever taken. In fact, he wasn't lying. Sergi was delighted with the new lifestyle that put money in his pocket without having to join in with his cousins' thuggish behaviour and gave him all the time in the world to play his sax and enjoy sex with Marisol.

Nine months later, Sergi showed his uncle a (fake) diploma that credited him with top marks in the exam. Pleased with the good return on his investment, Senyor Benito congratulated him profusely and then asked him to show what he had learned at the academy by opening him an account in a tax-free paradise.

"My lawyer says it's very easy, that you only need the internet and to know how to work a computer," he added, seeing the sceptical expression on his nephew's face.

"You know, Uncle, it's not so easy as that …"

"Come off it. They must have taught you this kind of thing on your course, right?"

"Well, not exactly …"

Sergi tried to explain to his uncle that tax evasion via a computer and internet connection was more complicated than he thought. It was one thing to be able to use Excel or Word, reboot your computer when it jammed or to use an anti-virus program and eliminate cookies and unnecessary files, but it was something else to open an offshore account in what his uncle called a tax-free paradise from your dining room, as if tax havens were like shopping at online Ikea.

Senyor Benito hadn't a clue what Sergi was talking about, and lost his temper.

"So what the fuck have you been doing all this time?! Do you mean I've been wasting my money?"

"No, Uncle, of course you haven't."

Sergi was terrified. Senyor Benito didn't realize the short course had cost him the equivalent of three years' fees in the Faculty of Medicine, and if he ever found out that Sergi had pocketed the monthly instalments but hardly gone to any classes, he'd be so annoyed he'd give him a facelift and break every bone in his body. Sergi kept inventing excuses, but when it looked like the old patriarch would rush off to the academy with his shotgun and scare the life out of the director because his nephew was so clueless, he said he'd look into it and see what he could do.

*

A couple of days later, Sergi went to see his uncle, equipped with the MacBook he'd persuaded him to buy for him while he was (theoretically) attending his computer course.

"Where do you want me to open the account, Uncle?" he enquired as he switched his computer on. "Switzerland? Or the Cayman Islands?"

"Panama," the old patriarch decreed. "I've heard that's where the most important people keep their cash. Do you know what rate of interest you get in Panama?"

"These tax havens," improvised Sergi as he keyed something into a document he'd previously prepared at home with a template and photos he'd found on Google, "don't pay interest. They just keep your money. You don't pay any taxes, obviously, and that's the joy of it. In fact, it's as if you were keeping your money in a mattress, but with someone keeping an eye on it 24/7."

"Oh!"

Sergi printed out the document and gave it to his uncle. You could see a bank logo next to the heading, "El Panameño", consisting of the silhouette of a pink flamingo. Underneath was what looked like an account number, and other figures that really meant nothing at all. Sergi hadn't put himself out looking for a name and a logo. Looking online, he had discovered there was a small island by the name of Flamenco, and the name had immediately made him think of The Flamingo, the most famous of the casinos set up by the Mafia in Las Vegas. He just couldn't resist having fun using the bird as the logo of a bank that didn't even exist.

"When can I start putting money into the account?" asked Senyor Benito, his eyes flashing impatiently.

"Tomorrow. First, I've got to organize an appointment with a bank middleman, who'll make sure the money reaches the branch."

The old patriarch looked happy enough. "Let me know when you've got the meeting, and I'll come and pick you up in the Mercedes."

The following morning Senyor Benito stuffed seven hundred thousand euros in wads of used notes into a backpack and drove Sergi to a bar on Barcelona's Carrer Muntaner. Senyor Benito rarely ventured into the city, and he knew that his appearance – his gypsy sideburns, imperial T-shirt, braces, straw boater and the oxygen bottle he was forced to cart around because of his emphysema – might catch certain people's eyes in some parts of the capital. His nephew asked him to stay inside his car, shotgun at the ready in case there was a problem. Sergi had donned his Sunday best in order not to look out of place among all the executives in suits and ties, and walked into the bar, emerging a few minutes later without the backpack. He handed his uncle a sheet of paper in the form of a bank statement which recorded a deposit of €685,000, all certified with a signature and stamp.

"The missing €15,000 is down to the bank and middleman's commissions," Sergi told his uncle, watching for his reaction out of the corner of his eye.

"I expected there'd be a cost," nodded Senyor Benito. "But, you know, I thought it'd be a lot more."

Sergi cursed silently (he'd not been sure what to pocket in terms of fees) and asked his uncle to get going. He had to go back to the bar and tie up a few loose ends with the middleman, he told him, as regards future transactions, and then he wanted to go to Decathlon and buy Marisol a present. Pleased with a receipt which registered that he now belonged to the millionaires' club with accounts in a tax haven, he blessed his bright idea of paying for his nephew to go on that computer course and told his driver (one of his brothers-in-law) to head off back to La Mina. Sergi, who'd told the bartender he'd gone out for a smoke, went back in, finished his beer and retrieved the backpack with the money. Then he caught a bus to Plaça de Catalunya and a train to Sant Adrià.

Back home, he put the €15,000 he'd decided to pocket into an envelope which he deposited in his bedside table drawer. He immediately picked up his backpack and drew the curtains. He used scissors to undo one of the seams in the mattress, gouged out a hole in the latex and stuffed in the rest of the money. Then he resealed the mattress with a stapler and eased it into the protective cover he'd had the forethought to buy in Carrefour to ensure Marisol didn't see the repairs, should she ever change the sheets.

He'd given the matter a lot of thought, but hadn't come up with a better place to hide the wads of notes.

And he had eventually concluded that years ago people must have had a good reason to keep their savings in their mattresses.

For months Senyor Benito continued to transfer money into the account he thought he had in Panama. The procedure was always the same: the patriarch drove his nephew to a bar in the upper reaches of Barcelona (always a different one), and Sergi would go in with a backpack or sports bag. Once inside, he'd order a beer and leave his leather jacket and bag for all to see. A few minutes later he'd go outside, ostensibly for a smoke, and hand his uncle the statement accrediting the transaction and a copy of the bank details showing the account balance. After he had watched the Mercedes disappear into the distance, he'd return to the bar, leave a handsome tip and retrieve his jacket and bag with the money.

Sometimes, it was the reverse operation: Senyor Benito would need cash and Sergi would be forced to undo the mattress and extract the required amount. Extracting money was more complicated, because he had to make up little bundles of notes, tape them to his legs and around his middle and, once inside the bar, go into the bathroom, put the money into a backpack (that he also had to carry incognito) and hand it to his uncle with the corresponding statement. Luckily, cash transfers were more frequent than withdrawals, because the operation to remove the little wads was extremely painful and Sergi was hard pressed not to yell out in the bathroom.

Senyor Benito's business was going so well that Sergi had to refurbish one of his rooms as a guest bedroom to have an excuse to justify to Marisol the purchase of a new double bed and mattress. The mattress of the bed where they slept had become too small to accommodate the envelopes his uncle kept passing on, to the point that Marisol complained the bed was so lumpy she found it uncomfortable. Marisol was surprised that Sergi had decided to dispense with the soundproof bedroom where he practised his sax, especially when she reflected that Sergi never had any guests to stay, but as she didn't want to be a control freak or give him any reason to poke his nose into *her* affairs, she didn't say a word.

From the day he was forced to open the phantom account in Panama for his uncle, Sergi was constantly on edge, nervously keeping an eye on his mattresses. He hardly slept a wink, and was so afraid he'd be burgled that he was always on the alert, since he never now slept in Marisol's flat and rarely saw his friends. Sergi didn't live in La Mina but on the other side of Besòs, and he'd realized that being related to one of the most feared gangsters in San Adrià was no protection against the foreign gangs that burgled flats in his area. He was scared stiff, and what with his lack of sleep, he was becoming paranoid.

Quite unintentionally, Sergi had become a bank. And the responsibility for watching over his uncle's savings night and day was souring his life.

*

Marisol issued an ultimatum: "You either come on holiday with me, or we're finished." She had noticed something was wrong with her boyfriend, but she couldn't get to the bottom of it. Sergi never wanted to go out, and, when they had a date, he always found excuses to stay in his flat, when she would grumble, "You know, you're like an old man, always stuck in front of the TV!" Marisol couldn't work out what was wrong, but she put Sergi's lethargy down to the heat and hoped a holiday away from it all, with plenty of fucks and paellas, would clear the air and restore his spirits.

Sergi knew it was absurd to fall out with his girlfriend and to spend all August shut up without air condition-ing in his flat because of those mattresses, and finally, after much agonizing, he agreed to go on holiday to Tenerife. While Marisol organized the hotel and flights and packed their cases, Sergi rang all his friends and acquaintances hoping that someone would do him a favour and stay in his flat while he was away, but at that time of summer he found no one. Feeling desperate, he almost asked his mother; but, as he knew his mother liked to scavenge and hoard, he realized that, on his return, he would find his flat had been redecorated with thousands of objects from rubbish containers, with their attendant insects, and quickly dropped the idea. Even so, before leaving he hung up a sign (that he'd previously stolen from a neighbouring house) to the effect that the residence was protected by a well-known security agency. The sign lasted a day and a half, the time it took his third-floor neighbours' adolescent son to tear it down.

Their holiday, in a five-star hotel on Tenerife, was a disaster. Sergi was so worried about the money in the mattresses that he didn't eat or sleep, and the mojitos Marisol forced him to gulp down upset his stomach and gave him palpitations. He didn't dare tell her how he'd fucked up – he'd have to give too many explanations, from his criminal ancestry to the delinquent nature of the family business – and the stress was lethal. By the third day, nerves had brought on a rash and his skin was covered in red blotches. Finally, anxiety affected his libido, and that also irritated Marisol.

"It would be OK if you couldn't get it up once, but we've had a week of no-shows, honey!"

When they returned from Tenerife, Marisol was more tanned and Sergi thinner. After they left the airport, Sergi accompanied Marisol home, where he didn't even get out of the taxi but headed straight off to Sant Adrià, where he saw that his door had been smashed in. The stress that had prevented him from enjoying the exotic landscapes of Tenerife and Marisol's caresses had been more than justified.

"You idiot, idiot, idiot …"

They'd broken in and burgled his flat. While he tried to stop his heart behaving like a second-hand clothes drier on full spin and got the air circulating through his lungs again, Sergi hoped against hope that the intruders had only lifted his plasma television, sound system, MacBook and the two thousand euros he'd barely hidden as a kind of bait to catch a putative thief (who would exclaim "Bingo!"). But what was on offer was far too tempting, thought Sergi, when he saw the mess in the dining room, and immediately realized he'd been visited by meticulous professionals who had scrutinized every millimetre of his flat from top to bottom. The TV, MacBook, sax and other valuable items had disappeared, and the mattresses had been ripped open and the money taken.

Sergi was in despair. At the very least, his uncle had lost some six million euros. And he knew that his uncle hadn't got to be who he was in Sant Adrià by being merciful and magnanimous when his subordinates put a foot wrong. If he found out about the fraudulent computer academy, the non-existent account in Panama and the wretched mattresses, he'd end up kneecapped or disembowelled in some backstreet. He'd fucked up big time. It was all over.

For a moment, Sergi was tempted to grab his suitcase, beat it and catch the first train that was heading far, far away, but he had second thoughts. Apart from being broke, he didn't know where to go. Besides, if he suddenly disappeared, his uncle would decide he had stolen the Panama money and would move heaven and earth to find him. His death would be a slow one, knowing his uncle; it would be preceded by a long, painful session with all kinds of pincers, saws, knives and soldering irons. Not to mention Marisol, who, in retaliation, might end up gagged and beaten to a pulp in some dark alleyway, being forced to answer questions she didn't understand and to which she'd have no answer.

Scarpering wasn't an option, thought Sergi.

But he'd have to invent something if he didn't want to end up in the cemetery.

It was a few days before Senyor Benito got back from his village. He did so the first week in September, furious because he'd had to drag Paco and Manel out of the cells after they'd had a skirmish with some musicians at a rave. Though he'd been dreading his uncle's call for days, Sergi's heart sunk when he heard his gravelly voice at the other end of the line.

"Are you in Sant Adrià? You're back from Tenerife?" he asked.

"Yes …"

"That's great. Some Russians have asked me to join in an operation, and I need a quarter of a million from my account in Panama to invest in the job."

"Are you sure it's a good idea to get mixed up with the Russians?" piped Sergi in a thin little voice.

"It won't be the first time we've collaborated, and the Russians have always kept their word so far," replied Senyor Benito, who added: "I know they're an odd bunch, but so are all foreigners, right?"

"I suppose so."

"Make the necessary calls. I'll come to pick you up early this afternoon. Don't keep me waiting."

And he hung up.

*

At four on the dot, Senyor Benito's Mercedes parked in front of the block of flats where his nephew lived. It was a muggy day, but the layer of arctic sweat coating Sergi's body was because he was scared stiff, and had nothing to do with the weather. He saw two Asian-looking men in the back of the car and his brain switched into panic mode.

"Uncle, I … Let me explain …" he spluttered, convinced his uncle had found out about the break-in and contracted two killers to do him in.

"They're Chinese," interrupted his uncle, who had opted to sit in the front seat. "They have a little job to do in Sarrià, but first they've got to go via Santa Coloma and get one of our cars so they can drive around Barcelona." (One of Senyor Benito's lines was buying and selling stolen cars with fake number plates.) "Chong" – the leader of one of the gangs Senyor Benito had allied himself with in the neighbourhood – "has asked me to take them, because they can't handle the metro and you can't trust taxi drivers." Before Sergi could say a word, he whispered: "I reckon they don't understand Catalan, but just in case, better wait till we've dropped them in Santa Coloma before we talk about our business. You never know with the Chinese."

"Fair enough."

Senyor Benito seemed in a good mood. "So how did your holidays go? Did you and Marisol have a good time?" he asked.

"You know, Tenerife is very nice, but nothing to write home about."

Senyor Benito cracked a joke, saying he didn't look very tanned after a beach holiday so he guessed he'd spent the whole trip shafting Marisol. Sergi concealed the feeling of humiliation that particular suggestion triggered and stared blankly out of the window.

"*Biutiful* Barcelona, right?' he asked the man with an equally blank expression who was sitting next to him.

It was a quarter of an hour's drive from Sant Adrià to the abandoned warehouse on the outskirts of Santa Coloma de Gramenet. The chauffeur stopped the car, the men got out and Senyor Benito took advantage of the change to sit next to Sergi.

"We'd better get a move on, because I've got to meet the Russians at six. Where do we have to drive this time?"

Sergi took two deep breaths.

"Uncle, I have to tell you something …"

"What's the matter?"

"The money in Panama has gone. The bank took it."

"What do you mean, 'the bank took it'?"

"You know, banks are a load of thieves," Sergi went on, apologetically. "It's a bit like what happened with that pyramid selling, except it happened in Panama and investors have lost all their money."

"Everything?"

"Brexit is clearly to blame," Sergi added, grim-faced.

"Brexit?" Senyor Benito furrowed his brows. "What the hell has Brexit got to do with Panama and my money?"

"It's all to do with the collapse of the City of London. The international markets have lost it, you know, as nobody knows what the repercussions might be when the UK leaves Europe. As all economies are now connected —"

"The fucking English … Never did like them! They come here, get drunk, get as pink as prawns, jump off balconies, and spend sod all … And drink so many *pintas* they don't have time to sniff … I do very little business with Englishmen. Let alone Englishwomen, who all dress as if they were whores!"

"Maybe we'll get something back over time …" Sergi suggested. "But for now, don't get your hopes up, Uncle. Look what happened to the banks. They lost investors' money, were given millions by the government and not a single director has ended up in jail."

"It's a scandal. Can't trust a soul these days!"

"Too right!"

Senyor Benito was beside himself. He wanted blood and guts, people hung, drawn and quartered, but Sergi managed to persuade him there was no point catching a plane and turning up at his bank's headquarters in Panama brandishing a shotgun. What's more, he added, his contacts had warned him that his bank was in Interpol's sights and if he personally went to ask for his money back, they'd arrest him for tax evasion and put him in the slammer.

"And, believe me, the clink in Panama is nothing like here …" Sergi was quick to add. "The Model was a five-star hotel compared to prisons over there."

"So what am I supposed to do now? Where should I keep my money?" Senyor Benito asked, beside himself.

"If you like, I can look into opening an account in Switzerland ..."

Senyor Benito hesitated a few seconds before he replied.

"You know what, Sergi? I reckon we should forget all this tax haven malarkey and go back to the old tried and tested system."

"What system, uncle?"

"Stuffing our money in our mattresses."

Mansion with Sea Views

Rafael knew Ahmed was no fool, but he also knew that he wouldn't dare go to the police.

Ahmed, a corpulent, curly-haired Moroccan who had been working for him for years, had found the bones when preparing the ground to erect a timber and stainless-steel railing designed to prevent anyone falling head first over the cliff. The brick wall that encircled the garden and acted as a barrier was low and in poor condition, and Antoni, whose mother was the owner, had asked Rafael to replace it with a modern fence as part of the general upgrade. It was a typical two-storey construction from the end of the sixties, located between Tamariu and Llafranc and overlooking the sea from the top of a steep precipice. It was a dangerous, fifteen-metre vertical drop, which gave the tenants of the currently uninhabited house spectacular views of the horizon and Costa Brava. They always grandly referred to it as their mansion.

When he'd demolished the low wall, Ahmed had also destroyed an exuberant hydrangea bush that Antoni's mother had first planted when he was a child, and it was there, under the flowers, that his spade had hit against bone. As soon he realized what he was digging up weren't the plant's roots but looked more like fragments of a human skeleton, Ahmed had taken fright and gone to get his boss.

Rafael was inside the house inspecting the layout of the plumbing and went to have a look, convinced that Ahmed was going loopy.

"They're only dog's bones!" he'd responded, in order to calm him down and laugh the matter off.

Ahmed, however, had naively stuck to his opinion.

"What do you mean, Senyor Rafael? I think they're a human being's …"

"No, they're not. They belong to the family's pet dog, you can be sure of that. You know what? Why don't you take the Transit and go and get some more tiles from the warehouse, because I reckon we're going to run out soon."

"What? Go to Barcelona now?"

Ahmed's tone of voice was a touch impertinent.

"Yes, you bet. And take Hassan with you to help."

Rafael was no expert, but he had immediately seen that Ahmed was right: the bones he'd dug up were human. When he saw them, he'd had a premonition, one of those that augur nothing good, and that was why, before getting on the telephone to tell the *mossos* about the find, he wanted to remove Ahmed and his mate from the scene.

"Do you want us back this afternoon with the material?" Ahmed asked.

Rafael looked at his watch. It was half past one.

"No, don't bother. But leave the Transit all set up so you can leave early in the morning."

"You're in charge, boss."

Rafael waited till he heard the van drive off before picking up the spade and beginning to dig.

The skull soon appeared, together with a rusty knife and a battered, putrefying leather suitcase that contained the rotted remains of what in their day must have been items of clothing.

"Shit …"

Rafael left the spade by the side of the pile of earth around the grave and, as best he could, squeezed past. He had no doubt that the bones belonged to Antoni's father, who had disappeared from his home forty years ago. The presence of a knife indicated that it had been a murder, and the fact he had been buried in his garden suggested that Antoni's mother was implicated. After all, it could hardly be a coincidence she had decided to plant a hydrangea bush right on the spot where her husband was buried, now, could it?

If he had put two and two together, so would the *mossos*.

Poor Antoni …

Antoni's father had disappeared from his own home on a Sunday in May 1974. When his wife informed the police, she had stated that money, a suitcase and several items of clothing belonging to her husband had also gone missing. As a result of that information, the detectives reached the conclusion that the man had abandoned his family by the back door, presumably to escape a boring marriage and seek his fortune somewhere in Latin America. It wouldn't be the first time, given that in the seventies divorce wasn't available and, that without the internet and DNA evidence, it was relatively simple to vanish into thin air. In the case of Antoni's father, the police had taken it for granted that he'd gone of his own free will and they hardly bust a gut looking for him. They had enough headaches at the time chasing opponents of the regime to worry about the disappearance of a harmless local shopkeeper who had no political profile or criminal record.

It had been the night before Antoni's seventh birthday when his father disappeared. He and Rafael were the same age (forty-six), had been born in the same neighbourhood on the right of the Eixample, and had studied at the same Catholic school run by Claretian priests on Carrer Pare Claret. Antoni's parents had run a small grocery shop near the Passeig de Sant Joan, very close to where Rafael lived, and as kids, when they came out of school, Rafael often went there and stayed to play in the back of the shop until his mother came to fetch him. Over the years, their lives had followed different paths – Antoni would become a writer and Rafael followed in his father's footsteps as a builder – but, one way or another, they had always kept in contact. As Rafael now owned one of those small construction companies that had proliferated before the crisis, when Antoni decided to sell the mansion he immediately thought of his friend as the best one to take a look and give him advice on the work to be done before they put it on the market.

The mansion had been shut up for at least ten years, and had never been refurbished. Health problems had forced Antoni's mother to stop going there in the summer, and Vero and Eulàlia, Antoni's wife and daughter, preferred to holiday in the flat Vero had inherited from her parents in Cadaqués, where the majority of their friends spent the summer. The mansion only generated expenses because it was in such a state of disrepair it was impossible to rent and make money out of. The plastic and Formica that were fashionable at the time and which they'd used to embellish the bathrooms had fallen apart and the stippling Antoni's father had insisted on using everywhere gave the place a faux rustic, tawdry look. The electrical fittings and plumbing were also a problem, and, like the roof, were responsible for the damp and mildew on the walls and ceilings.

"It looks decrepit," was Rafael's verdict. "If you really want to make money, you'll have to refurbish it from top to bottom."

Rafael persuaded Antoni it was worthwhile investing money in a proper revamp before putting the house on the market. He himself had sketched out a plan to convert the modest late-sixties construction into a desirable luxurious summer residence with open spaces and minimalist design of the kind featured in glossy interior design and architecture magazines. As Antoni wasn't in a position to take on the necessary investment, they had come to an agreement: Rafael would advance the money to buy materials and would expect to be paid when Antoni managed to sell the mansion. They would both make money and what's more, Rafael could use the project for promotional purposes, after the crisis had almost bankrupted him.

Rafael was startled by the cries of a famished seagull passing overhead. His gaze instinctively sought refuge in the expanse of salt water and his eyes were filled with an insipid haze of greys and blues, the colours of the day's dawn. He zipped up his jacket and stuffed his hands into his pockets, trying to warm himself up. Why the hell had he ever asked Ahmed to knock down that wall? How could he be so unlucky?

He covered the ditch with a sheet of plastic in case it rained and went back into the house. He wasn't one to drink – only the odd drop at parties or with friends – but he now decided that a whisky or cognac would help him find the courage to handle the two calls he had to make, to the *mossos* and to Antoni, so he rummaged in the kitchen cupboards hoping he'd find a bottle. He didn't. The only option was to drive to Tamariu, the nearest town, where he could buy a packet of Marlboros and smoke that cigarette he'd been dreaming of for over five years.

As soon as he reached Tamariu he went to the Passeig, where he recalled seeing the only bar on the promenade that was open out of season. After parking his car, he went in, bought a packet of cigarettes and a lighter and ordered a beer – at that time of day, with an empty stomach, he was afraid a whisky or cognac might upset him – and told the waitress, a girl whose accent and looks seemed eastern European, that he would smoke his cigarette on the terrace.

Helped by the beer, the cigarette unleashed an avalanche of forgotten sensations and made him feel slightly queasy, but he lit up a second right away. He couldn't stop thinking how different things would be if he hadn't asked Ahmed to knock down the brick wall to replace it with railings and his spade hadn't hit those remains. Antoni wouldn't have to suffer the torment of discovering that his mother was a murderer who had been deceiving him for a lifetime, and he wouldn't be about to lose out on the investment he had made when paying for the materials for the house refurbishment out of his own pocket.

All in all, a fucking disaster.

Subdued by alcohol and nicotine, Rafael calculated that he'd not seen Antoni's mother for fifteen years. He knew she still lived by herself in the flat where she had lived forever, above the grocery shop, but lately his friend had told him her health was rather delicate and she'd been forced to employ a young woman to help with the housework. She didn't get on with Vero, her daughter-in-law, but Antoni still worshipped his mother, who had brought him up as a single parent at a time when the servile values inculcated by the Feminine Section of the Falange were still in vogue and women were the first to criticize or find failings in wives who were mistreated or abandoned by their husbands.

The knife he had seen next to the skeleton indicated that the man had been stabbed to death. What on earth could have happened? Had it been an attack in a moment of passion, or a premeditated crime? Whatever the case, if she *had* killed him, somebody must have helped her, thought Rafael, because Antoni's mother was on the small side and clearly didn't have the strength to drag a corpse the size and weight of Antoni's father the length of the garden. Rafael recalled that there had been an uncle, Antoni's mother's brother, who sometimes fetched him from school. Was he the one who had helped? Or perhaps there had been another man, a lover nobody knew about? However, Antoni's mother had never remarried or had any other relationship, at least as far as he knew. A female lover, perhaps, in those times when women rarely came out of the closet? He didn't think so.

Rafael lit a third cigarette. Antoni's mother was the only one who could answer all these questions. Would they put her in prison, at her age? And how would Antoni react when he realized that the man he had hated all his life wasn't a good-for-nothing who had abandoned him but the victim of a crime? Rafael was worried by the turmoil the find would plunge his friend into, but he also fretted over the impact it would have on his own family. If the refurbishments were stopped, he wouldn't be able to pay his suppliers and would have to file for bankruptcy. He would lose his company. And, at his age, with the crisis the building industry had suffered, he would find it difficult to find work anywhere.

Besides, he was dreading communicating the find to the *mossos*. A couple of months ago, the foreign woman with whom he had enjoyed the only extramarital affair he'd had in twenty years of married life had committed suicide in the bathtub he had just installed in her flat in Sarrià and he'd had to answer loads of questions. Of course, he'd had nothing to do with the death of that idiotic Englishwoman and nobody had suggested any such thing, but what would happen if the police found it suspicious when another corpse appeared linked to his name and, one way or another, his wife found out that he had cheated on her?

There was another option. To do nothing. Or rather, to pretend that none of it had happened. Take the bones, hide them somewhere else and not tell anybody.

In fact, he knew the perfect place to hide them.

After so many years …

There was a village not far from Olot that went by the name of Campfredor, the birthplace of Rafael's mother, where he and his siblings had spent their childhood Easter and summer holidays. Located in one of the inaccessible valleys of the Alta Garrotxa, Campfredor had been spared the pressure of tourism thanks to a road that was more like a mountain track and which, when it snowed in winter, left the inhabitants of the village isolated from the rest of civilization and, most importantly, from the ski resorts. Campfredor hardly figured on maps, and Rafael reckoned it would take him a couple of hours to get there. He'd better get a move on if he didn't want night to fall first.

He paid for his beer, went to get his car and drove back to the house. Ahmed and Hassan kept all the tools and building materials on the ground floor, and he soon found the black plastic sacks they used for rubbish. He grabbed a couple, and some work gloves, and headed to the grave. Fortunately, the mansion was separated from the road by a pine copse, and, as it was a weekday, there were no summer holidaymakers in the neighbouring houses who might be tempted to pry.

Helped by the gloves and spade, he lifted the bones into one of the sacks and the suitcase and knife into the other. The next morning, he would tell Ahmed he had dug up the dog himself and dumped the remains in a rubbish container. He was sure that Ahmed and Hassan wouldn't swallow any of that, but neither would they ask any questions or think of telling the police. Even though their papers were in order, they were still third-category foreigners, below immigrants from Europe and people who professed a religion other than Islam. Rafael knew they wouldn't create problems for themselves by notifying the police about the discovery of an old skeleton on the building site where they were working.

He put the sacks, gloves and spade in the car boot and headed off to Campfredor. The place he was looking for was on the outskirts of the village, in a spinney that was difficult to reach, which he had discovered years ago by pure chance. The track there was narrow and sloping, and he had to walk the last stretch. When it became too narrow, Rafael got out of his car, grabbed the sacks, spade and torch, and started walking along a stony, overgrown path. At most he reckoned he had half an hour of light left. When he reached the wood, he carried on till he found what he was looking for: a huge oak tree with tangled branches that stood out from the other trees because of its thick trunk.

Rafael moved slightly away from the tree and started digging. It must have rained recently, because the ground was soft. Even so, the operation to dig a big enough hole took longer than he had anticipated, and, when he'd finished the job, the sky was already a dark shade of twilight and the wood had been transformed into a series of hostile shadows. Rafael stuck the sacks in the hole, next to each other, and then refilled the hole with earth. Just in case, he scattered several spadefuls of dry leaves on top to hide his excavations.

Before going back to his car, he walked as far as the oak tree that had been his point of reference and leaned back against the south-facing side of the trunk. He took twenty paces, stopped, and by the light of his torch cleared away the undergrowth until he found three rocks the size of footballs half-hidden amid the ferns. They were still there, in a row, covered in moss, after all those years. It didn't look as if a soul had touched them.

Desirée was buried under those stones, an eighteen-year-old French hitchhiker he had given a lift to on the road from Olot to Campfredor. Rafael had invited her to get into his car, and, when he stuck his hand between her thighs, searching for her sex, the little whore had moved away, said no and told him to stop the car and let her get out. He had chased her into the wood, grappled with her and thrown her to the ground. During the struggle, while he held her by the wrists, unzipped her shorts and tried to pull her knickers down, the girl's head had struck a rock and she'd stopped breathing. She'd died there and then. And he could do nothing, except bury her in those woods.

He wasn't to blame. It had been an accident. And, at the end of the day, she had been the one who'd asked him to stop the car and had provoked him with her hot pants and plunging neckline. As if he hadn't known what she really wanted …

Because he was no rapist.

That was one thing he was sure of.

He listened to the radio on the way back. When he reached home, it was almost nine o'clock and had just started to rain. His wife was in the kitchen getting dinner ready, and his son was shut in his bedroom, as he was every night, watching videos, listening to music or playing with his tablet. There was still time.

It was time to celebrate, yet again, that everything had turned out fine.

And with an easy conscience induced by the feeling of a job well done, Rafael went into the dining room, sat on their sofa and slowly smoked the last cigarette in the packet.

I Detest Mozart

I detest Mozart. His music seriously gets on my nerves. Naturally I also don't like Verdi, Rossini, Handel, Monteverdi, Puccini or Bellini or Wagner ... In a nutshell, I can't stand opera. Even though I undoubtedly belong to the select band of old-timers who have watched the most performances at the Liceu.

I was born in 1924 and have been going to that opera house since I was eighteen. I am now ninety-two. I don't think I have missed a single premiere in all those years or that there is a single divo or diva I haven't heard sing. You will probably regard this as a privilege, but I can tell you, as far as I'm concerned, going to the Liceu has always been a torture. And then you will ask: if she doesn't like opera, why has this good lady spent half her life going to the Liceu? Well, you know, once upon a time things weren't that easy.

I'm referring to people of our social standing.

The first time I went to the opera, it was with my parents. I had just had my eighteenth birthday and had celebrated my coming out at a big party in the house where we then lived on Passeig de la Bonanova, and Mama thought I was now of an age to go to the Liceu to see an adult performance. I had never been, and naturally enough I was thrilled at the idea of going out at night and dressing up for the theatre. In those days when almost everything was banned, there was very little in the way of entertainment, and the only distractions on hand were going to mass or the dressmaker's, or doing charity work.

Mama, who was very clever, didn't choose any ordinary day to take me; she decided on a night at the end of January when a gala performance was planned in honour of the Generalísimo that would bring together the city's great and good. In those days, our family belonged to an exclusive circle of politicians, military, bankers and businessmen, and, as the daughter of one of the country's most important Catalan industrialists, I had to experience the rite of initiation of a night at the Liceu and being paraded in all my finery before my peers. You can't imagine *how* excited I was! I had never attended a big society event or seen Franco in the flesh – Papa was full of praise for the man – and I was so nervous I lost my appetite. We're talking about the year 1942. The war that had forced us to leave Barcelona and set up home in Camprodon to escape the anarchist gunmen had only finished three years ago.

The programme to pay homage to the Caudillo comprised the first and second acts of *Madame Butterfly* and the second act of *Lohengrin*. Mama was passionate about

Wagner, whom she believed to be much superior to Verdi, and was of the opinion that *Lohengrin* was an excellent choice. Wagner's music was epic and patriotic, she said, like the decimation of the reds that Franco had pursued to protect us from communism and the "Jewish–Masonic conspiracy". I think I had heard the occasional piece by Puccini and Wagner on the radio at home, but never a whole opera (I don't even recall whether they broadcast operas in those days), and, whenever I had the choice, I preferred piano concertos by Beethoven or Schubert that were more in tune with the state of mind of the young girl I was at the time: an eighteen-year-old innocent who went to mass in the morning and enjoyed secret fantasies of Errol Flynn by night.

That evening the Liceu looked splendid, so brightly lit and bedecked with flowers. The façade had been covered in small lights, as if it were Christmas, and the entrance had been decorated with plants and bay trees. I too looked gorgeous, in a full-length sky-blue satin dress Mama had had made specially, with sparkling jewels and gauze ruffs that covered my thin arms. I was a skinny young thing – Mama was always complaining food never seemed to fill me out – and in those post-war times with so many sick and starving, spindly girls weren't fashionable as they are now and we were forced to hide the scant flesh on our bones to avoid people jumping to the conclusion that we were suffering from tuberculosis.

The performance began at a quarter past nine. Even though it was the usual damp cold January on the Rambla and at the front of the Boqueria market, the crowds were packed tight behind the barriers the police had erected around the theatre and were fervently shouting out the name of the Generalísimo and the traditional "*Viva España!*" The Liceu's lobby was also full of people and quite a spectacle with men in their tuxedos and glittering, bejewelled women who, like us, added a touch of colour with their brand-new gala outfits. The audience also contained lots of military in dress uniforms resplendent with medals, and one of them, a colonel who was a friend of Papa, told me it was a soldier, the Marquis of Mina, who had brought opera to Barcelona in the last century and turned it into the city's favourite musical form. I already knew that, because the teacher who egregiously failed to teach me to play the piano had told me; however, I was polite, said nothing and simply smiled sweetly as I listened to his lengthy explanations.

Our seats gave us a magnificent view of the presidential box located in the centre of the dress circle. They had adorned it with flowers and a big tapestry, and, as the moment when the performance was to start drew near, all eyes focused on that part of the theatre expecting Franco to appear, but he didn't. To my astonishment, the curtain went up and the orchestra began although neither the Generalísimo nor his wife were present. I was totally flummoxed. How could Franco arrive late to a function that had been organized in his honour? What could have happened?

When Franco finally entered the auditorium, accompanied by Doña Carmen, it was gone half past ten and we were over halfway through the first act of *Madame Butterfly*. As soon as they spotted him, the singers stopped singing and the orchestra switched from Puccini to a lively account of the first bars of the national anthem. Everybody rose to their feet, clapping and shouting: "Franco! Franco! Franco!" It was incredible. I remember how my heart beat so fast I thought for a moment I would faint and cut a foolish figure in front of all those people. The hero of the fatherland, the saviour of Spain in person. I saw how Mama, like many other ladies, shed tears while she applauded with her extremely elegant grey gloves.

That night, I had so many new exciting experiences, I hardly noticed what was happening onstage. Later on, when we were driving home, Papa asked me whether I had enjoyed the performance and I replied that I had, immensely. What else could I have said? Of course, it was a big mistake, because my parents concluded that I loved opera and, from that day onward, my life took a different path and I started to go regularly to the Liceu.

I soon discovered that opera was truly tedious. All that shrieking and screaming, and plots that were so tragic and entangled I found them hard to unravel ... Worst of all were the baroque composers, and, of course, Wagner, with his endless operas that went on for over five hours and were sung in German to boot. There were evenings when the performances were so drawn-out I couldn't keep still on my chair and Mama was forced to scold me. I couldn't help it: my bones stuck to the seat, and my posterior and legs went to sleep; I felt like a pincushion. And it went on for hours and hours! When I looked at the audience in the gods I could hardly believe that people existed who were willing to *stand* through a whole opera, and nobody was obliging them to do so. Papa, who was also bored out of his mind at the Liceu, said that the people in the gods were the true connoisseurs, and that the critics who wrote reviews for the daily newspapers took more notice of their applause or whistles than ours.

The only good thing about the Liceu was that afterwards we would go the Fonda Espanya for dinner. That was the bit I liked. Not so much for the food – I recognize that at the time I was very pernickety and, as Mama would say, I pecked at it like a sparrow – but because we always went with some of Papa's friends, who had sons my age. On one such soirée I met Pere, the older son of the Gelaberts, and I became totally infatuated. He was a handsome, engaging boy and much more fun than the sourpusses I usually had to converse with. Mama, who immediately noticed I was fixated on that young man, said right away that the Gelaberts didn't have sufficient status to be part of our family and killed dead any hopes I might have nurtured in that direction. I didn't dare disagree. I trusted her judgement, and, besides, Mama was very bad-tempered and under no circumstances did I want to annoy her.

Now and then, particularly in those early days, I was on the verge of confessing that I detested opera and that going to the Liceu was a real pain. But Mama was so proud – "Mercedes follows in my shoes. She *loves* the opera!" she liked to boast to her lady friends – that I didn't have the heart to tell her the truth. Going to the Liceu was a compulsory society activity for people of our social class, and if Mama had taught me one thing, it was that women in our position also had to make sacrifices. Life – even a life as comfortable as ours – wasn't all a bed of roses. There was a price to pay in order to have a good husband and live in a nice house, to own jewels, pretty dresses and have domestic servants and never to be forced to worry about anything as vulgar as money. It was a case of suffering in silence. And being patient. I hoped that, when I married, I would be able to stop going to the Liceu or, at least, would no longer have to go so often.

Early in December 1944, my paternal grandmother died of a heart attack. Mourning obliged us to wear black, and we didn't go to the Liceu for months. I discovered that was a good way to avoid having to go to the Rambla to listen to opera, and, even though I was saddened by grandmother's death, I was thankful she had passed away at the beginning of the opera season and not at the end. We missed almost every performance. When Mama decided that we could ease off on the mourning in the spring and we rejoined the social round, I was ready to pray to God with all my heart to remove another relative so I wouldn't have to go to the Liceu.

The trouble now was that we didn't just go to the opera, but to the ballet as well. Frankly, I don't know which was worse. I occasionally made an excuse and managed to stay at home. "My head really aches"; "It's that time of the month …" I would sometimes tell Mama. But I knew I couldn't overplay that card. My only source of consolation was the hope there would be another death in the family and we would don our mourning weeds once again.

Nonetheless, the months went by and none of my relatives seemed in a hurry to die. I was desperate. Although I did all I could to hide the fact, those soirées at the Liceu were endless and, while I was in our box, I spent every second wishing a disaster would occur so I could stay at home. I wanted a revolutionary to appear and throw another Orsini into the stalls, or another war to break out, or the Liceu to burn down …

I know I was taking things too far, but imagining such catastrophes was the only way I could keep awake during those interminable performances.

One Tuesday at the end of November 1945, I stayed at home with Grandfather, alone except for the girl who helped our maid with the laundry. I was feeling rather delicate and had decided to stay and daydream in my bedroom until lunchtime. I heard Grandfather call out.

"Merceeeè …! Please come and help me down the stairs. I want to go into the garden for a while."

"Won't you catch cold, Grandfather? You know how at this time of year —"

"But can't you see how sunny it is, my dear? Go and find Maria and she can help you, because you won't be able to handle me by yourself."

Grandfather was no invalid, but he found walking difficult and spent most of the time sitting in his wheelchair. He was elderly, and after Grandmother died he had come to live with us and been given one of the first-floor bedrooms. As there wasn't a lift, he had an invalid chair upstairs that enabled him to move along the passage and around his bedroom, and a second one on the ground floor. He needed to be helped by Father or one of our maids when he wanted to go up or downstairs.

"Mercè, why are you looking at me like that?"

I didn't think twice. Grandfather was sitting in his wheelchair next to the stone balustrade, and I pushed him downstairs with all my might.

"Merceeè—"

He bounced down to the bottom like a ball.

"Help! Grandfather has fallen downstairs and hurt himself!" I screamed.

The doctor said he had broken his neck and that death had been instantaneous. Of course, I was consoled to know he hadn't suffered. Everyone put Grandfather's fall down to a tragic accident; no questions were asked, no investigation was opened, it was an eminently reasonable assumption. Who would have ever thought that a sensitive young woman who wouldn't say boo to a goose might have pushed her grandfather downstairs so she could wear black and stop going to the Liceu?

Thanks to Grandfather I missed more than half the season that year.

"I'm so sorry for our little treasure," Mama lamented. "She so adores her nights at the opera …"

At about that time – I had just celebrated my twenty-first birthday – I had started courting Josep Maria, heir to the Margalló fortune. My parents had selected a young man who was the son of one of Papa's wealthiest partners and who, of course, was a member of the Liceu Circle. Josep Maria was fat, squat and spotty and his hands were always sweaty. I hated his presence near me, but Mama said that uniting our families would mean that Father's businesses would prosper even more and she assured me that the life of a grand dame that Josep Maria would bring me would more than compensate for having to keep him happy in bed.

All of a sudden I discovered that Josep Maria also detested the opera. Naturally, he didn't like dancing, the movies, bullfights or going out for aperitifs on a Sunday either – nothing at all, in fact. My God, he was so boring! Nevertheless, as we hardly knew each other and we wanted plain sailing when we were courting, I never dared tell him I too hated that kind of music and that, when we went to the Liceu, I found it tedious beyond belief. Even so, for a time I did think I had struck lucky with the fiancé my parents had chosen, and was convinced that, as he didn't like opera, after our marriage we would stop going to the Liceu or, at the very least, would only go now and then, to keep up appearances.

However, I couldn't have been more wrong.

*

Josep Maria's Mama, who was a widow, simply loved to go to the Liceu and show off her furs and jewels, and as soon as we were wed, her son slotted me into the ritual. Overnight I became her companion and we started going to the opera together. If going to the Liceu was already the height of tedium, I soon discovered it was frankly torture to do so with one's mother-in-law. Apart from having to listen to all those singers screeching hour after hour, in the intervals I now had to endure that lady's advice and criticism: I didn't know how to manage the servants, I spent too much or too little, I didn't eat the right things, I should be pregnant by now … And I was forced to turn the other cheek and say amen to everything, because Josep Maria doted on his mother and I knew that, if we argued, I would be the one to lose out.

Luckily at the time I could fall back on my cousin Mariona, the only real friend I have ever had. We were the same age and had grown up together, and she was the only person who knew how much I hated opera. One day, when she saw me looking suicidal, she advised me to pluck up courage and tell Josep Maria the truth.

I heeded her words, but it wasn't a good idea.

"So you have been deceiving people all this time, have you?!" snapped a furious Josep Maria when he learned of my secret.

"I'm really sorry. I said nothing initially because I didn't want to upset Mama and Papa. And later —"

"Well, it's too late now!" he retorted. "You have become a kind of institution at the Liceu. You do realize that, don't you? – 'Mrs Margalló is so knowledgeable, and never misses a first night …' – What do you think they'll say if you suddenly stop going?"

"But …"

"No ifs or buts … I'm not going to allow you to make a fool of me! You will continue to go to the Liceu and will never tell anyone what you have just told me. And I would like to remind you," he added in that tone he adopted when speaking to his subordinates, "I am the major shareholder in your father's company and, if it wasn't for me, his creditors would have taken him to the cleaners long ago!"

I had to swallow my tears and my pride.

And continue going to the Liceu.

Nevertheless, I didn't surrender. The loathing I felt towards my mother-in-law gave me the idea, and the endless hours I sat in our box allowed me to think up a scheme that would kill her off reasonably peacefully thanks to the foxgloves growing in our garden. Our gardener had warned me it was a dangerous plant, and one day, consulting some books in Papa's library, I discovered that one could make a poison from its leaves that left no trace: I got to work. Subsequently, my mother-in-law died from a heart attack provoked by an infusion of foxglove leaves and she was buried without even an autopsy.

Eighteen months later, my brother-in-law (a horrible chap, and as ugly as my husband) fell over a precipice in the course of a family excursion to the Turó de l'Home mountains, in circumstances that, on this occasion, the police did think were rather strange. That was when I realized I needed to put the brakes on. So many sudden deaths in the family, and in such quick succession, might arouse suspicion, and something everyone put down to a run of bad luck – "the Margallós, poor dears, can't seem to shake it off" – might lead to an investigation being opened that would cast a bad light on me. No more accidents or sudden illnesses, I decided. Whether I liked it or not, I would have to resign myself to going to the Liceu.

At the time – I must have been in my mid-thirties – I had already begun to fantasize about ridding myself of Josep Maria. While I was in our box, listening to those sopranos and tenors warbling away, I amused myself making plans and alibis, choosing poisons, pistols, axes and knives. It was really a harmless pastime I wasn't ever intending to put into practice, because, although it's true that Josep Maria's premature death would supply me with the perfect alibi never to be forced to listen to an opera again – "ay, Mercedes is so sad she has pledged to the Virgin of Montserrat that she will never again cross the threshold of the Liceu, she who so likes the opera …!" – Josep Maria saw to everything and I couldn't be sure that his death wouldn't have negative repercussions on our lifestyle. I still had three children to bring up and I had no idea how Josep Maria's business worked, and that inhibited me.

Besides, it's not so easy to find a way to kill a young man that doesn't arouse suspicion.

*

Towards the end of the eighties, my cousin Mariona died
in a fire in the house the family owned in Puigcerdà.
Her son and young daughter also lost their lives in the
disaster – only Montserrat, her granddaughter, was saved –
and that tragedy affected me deeply. From the moment
Franco died, everything really changed and I felt disori-
ented, and now, without Mariona, I had nobody left to
confide in. For a time I succumbed to what is now called
depression and turned into a recluse at home. Josep
Maria, who by now was one of the country's wealthiest
industrialists, decided I was play-acting and was furious:
he told me that I either snapped out of my depression
and fulfilled my social duties, or he would stick me into
an asylum. A couple of female acquaintances in my social
circle had ended up in the madhouse – one for the right
reasons, because she hallucinated and had tried to kill
her children; the other case wasn't so straightforward,
and I found the very idea quite terrifying.

In the event, I wasted no time when the occasion
presented itself. Josep Maria had always had an iron
constitution, but at the age of sixty-four his appendix was
perforated and he required an emergency operation.
There was a sofa bed in the room in the clinic and, as I
had had a brainwave, I offered to spend a night there to
provide him with some company.

It was child's play to lay my hands on a syringe and inject
a bubble of air through the drip supplying him serum.

And four years later, the Liceu burnt down.

By the way, that had nothing to do with me. Though I had toyed with the idea. Lamentably, it was rebuilt …

The first half must be about to begin. They are performing *The Twilight of the Gods*, one of Wagner's interminable operas that always give me a splitting headache. It is rather surprising that the English consul isn't here, because he is so fond of opera and never misses a first night. Unlike his wife, who rarely comes, because everybody knows she doesn't like opera and skives off whenever she can. She is *so* fortunate! If only I could follow suit … Because who'd have ever told me that, at my age, I would still have to go to listen to operas?

For over twenty years I've been coming to the Liceu in a wheelchair, ever since I had a stroke. A year after I buried Josep Maria, half of my body was paralysed and I was reduced to a completely invalid state. I can't speak, and as arthritis prevents me from using my good hand, I can't write either. I have no way of telling my grandson, Carlos, to please stop taking me to the Liceu because I detest opera. The darling does everything in good faith, and, unlike me, he loves the opera (Josep Maria and I always suspected poor Carlos preferred his carnations green). Whenever there is a premiere he drives round to pick me up, decks me out in my furs and jewels and takes me to the Liceu.

Now I am ninety-two, I no longer pray for someone else's death, but for God to take me as soon as He can. Even though I am slightly worried by the possibility that hell exists and that my punishment will be to sit in a theatre and listen to opera for the whole of eternity. As I can't speak and confess my sins to the priest, I don't know if the absolution he gives me will act to open St Peter's gates or if I will find them shut when I arrive.

If the truth be told, however much I try, I can never bring myself to repent for the evil deeds I have committed throughout my life to avoid all those nights at the opera.

May God have mercy …

Birds of a Feather

Juani accepted that they might have gone a bit too far with "posh pussy". "Watch out, we ain't got a clue who this bunny is. She seems very highfalutin, but she must have done something really serious to get shut up in here," she had warned them that first day. She had just seen the four inmates she shared a cell with at the Wad-Ras female prison crowd around the newcomer's locker and bed and start rummaging among her things and grabbing what they fancied. "And she'll know it were us," she added while she herself snaffled some Calvin Klein knickers and bras that still carried the price tags from the shop. Sarai, whose feet were always cold now she was menopausal, even in the summer, had pocketed flannel socks and a silk scarf; Candela had gone for the eau de cologne and gossip magazines; Daniela and Catina, the most make-up conscious, had fought over an incredibly expensive Shiseido anti-wrinkle cream that hadn't been opened. Daniela won out, a burly, brawny Colombian whose face was as wrinkled as a prune and who was a good foot taller than Catina. Catina, slight in build, a heroin addict originally from Bucharest, had to be satisfied with eyeliner and pink lipstick that didn't go with her chipped, blotchy teeth.

The five inmates had only just made the acquaintance of Montserrat Codina i Cadalfach, but they'd immediately registered that the new jailbird was not starving to death. She'd made her entry into the cell dragging a Samsonite suitcase behind her and wearing an Adidas backpack that didn't look as if it had fallen off the back of a lorry; her fancy Costa Brava tan, manicured nails, elaborate hairdo and designer tracksuit spoke for themselves. They were now sharing their room with a rich tart with two snobby Catalan surnames, and that was very peculiar indeed in Wad-Ras. Juani, who was naturally outgoing, had taken on the task of making introductions and giving her a welcome, but Montserrat smirked sourly in response, muttering only a faint "hello" to their "Hi, posh pussy!", and that didn't augur well.

"She don't look like no whore," commented Juani, who was familiar with the trade and known as Vanessa to her customers. "Hey, don't you be fooled by looks. I bet she's sucked a few cocks in her time," retorted Sarai. As they always did when a new inmate arrived, the five women laid bets: Juani and Daniela bet she'd been done for drug trafficking, the most popular crime in the prison; Candela and Catina plumped for high-class prostitution and fraud; only Sarai, who'd been put in the slammer for stabbing a girl who had flirted with her guy, was convinced it was due to something violent. "This sort," she said, referring to the social class she imagined Montserrat Codina came from, "only get put inside if they kill somebody."

The moment she got back from the interview that all new internees are obliged to have on their first day in prison, Montserrat Codina noticed they'd interfered with her belongings and that a handful of items had vanished. "Posh pussy, it's the dues you pay for being new," said Daniela, marking out the territory. "My name is Montserrat, not 'posh pussy'," replied Montserrat Codina in a tone they all felt to be much too sour. "And I'd appreciate it if you could return my things."

"What are you going to do, posh pussy, tell the cops? You can't imagine what we do to snitches here," rasped Sarai, walking towards her and flexing her muscles. The gypsy's defiant stance brought a round of laughter and applause from the rest of the inmates, and revealed horrendously hairy armpits that gave off a stink that quickly filled the room.

Montserrat Codina didn't shrink back. She stood her ground and stared hard into Sarai's eyes, making it clear that she wasn't intimidated by threats from any squat, smelly gypsy woman. When Sarai finally tired of trying to stare her out and went back to her bunk, Montserrat Codina turned around, took a book from her backpack and, with a winner's smarmy smile, stretched out on the bed she'd been assigned. The five inmates interpreted her silence and attitude as a challenge and insulted her. "Well, if posh pussy ain't a bleedin' brainbox!" joked Candela, reinforcing her comment with a loud, pungent belch.

Daniela, whose curiosity had been aroused, stood on tiptoes to read the book's title (Montserrat was in the top bunk farthest from the window, above Juani), but as it was written in German she couldn't understand what it said. As luck would have it, German didn't figure among the languages spoken in that multicultural Babel: Spanish, which served as the lingua franca; English, which Daniela and Catina spoke reasonably well; Catalan, which was understood by Sarai, Candela and Juani; Romanian, Catina's mother tongue; and finally Romany, which Candela and Sarai sometimes used to speak to each other.

Later, out in the yard, where they usually went for a while before going to eat, the five veteran inmates complained about how unlucky they'd been with the new prisoner who'd landed in their cell. What a pity she was such a stuck-up bitch … She'd weep soon enough at night, when it was lights out and she realized Wad-Ras wasn't exactly a luxury spa. When she began to miss all the nice things – they figured – she'd been used to, and got tired of rubbing herself off at night, with no men to stick their cocks deep inside her or lick her fanny … She'd lose her airs and graces and see she was nothing special. Who did she think she was?

At lunchtime Montserrat Codina sat by herself and ignored anyone who came over and tried to start a conversation. She ate the salad and beans on the menu that day without batting an eyelid, though she didn't touch the bread. After lunch, she went back to her cell, where she stayed while Sarai had a nap and the others watched the TV in the common room, walked round the yard or joined in some handicraft workshop.

"Fucking hell, what a bitch you've got there ... She's loaded, that's for sure," the other inmates told them.

The six women didn't get back together in their cell until the evening. Aware that they'd set off on the wrong foot, Juani took the initiative and tried to smooth things over by telling Montserrat Codina why they had been put inside: she'd got three years for selling heroin and other shit in the Raval district; Daniela, for entering the country with ten kilos of coke hidden in uncomfortable, unlikely places; Sarai and Candela were reoffenders and in for robbery and intimidation (additionally, Candela had been done for GBH, because the grandma whose bag she'd tried to steal had fallen down and broken a hip); Catina, who was the quietest and often seemed not quite all there, had been sentenced to years inside for drug trafficking and working with a gang of Romanians who, among other things, procured underage prostitutes for roadside soliciting.

Montserrat Codina merely listened to Juani's chatter and looked bored. When she finished and Candela asked Montserrat what she'd done to end up inside, she said that she'd done "something she shouldn't" and sank her head back into the pages of her book, making it quite clear she wasn't intending to tell them her life story or leave space for any camaraderie among thieves. Before lights out, Daniela and Sarai cracked a few more jokes at the expense of their arrogant new inmate, but as they didn't trigger any response, they soon gave up and ignored her.

That night, unusually for a newcomer to Was-Rad, Montserrat Codina didn't cry. And, as far as they knew, she didn't shed a single tear on subsequent nights.

Juani was the most sociable of the five women who shared cell 23 before Montserrat Codina showed up. She had been born in the Raval thirty-six years ago, when it was still called the *barrio chino*, where she'd been brought up by an Andalusian grandma who taught her to sing the songs of Doña Concha Piquer while her mother, a whore by profession too and an occasional petty thief to boot, entered La Trinitat prison more often than she left it. Juani had been jailed for drug trafficking, but being a mule was only one of her regular activities to bring in enough income to make up for the paltry sum her pimp handed her for opening her legs. Unlike most of her friends in the Raval, Juani wasn't hooked on any of the illegal substances that were hawked undercover in the neighbourhood of the Liceu, and was still pretty. She had a good rapport with the prison staff, which meant that, the following morning, she was given the job of extracting from one of the jailers the crime for which Montserrat Codina had been stuck in the slammer.

"None of us got it. She's in for five years for stashing money away in Switzerland," she later told her friends over lunch. "Switzerland, for Christ's sake. But you bet she's from a good family, and will soon get let out," Juani then added.

"She may be rude, but you can see she's got class," observed Daniela, struggling to hide her envy.

"You mean she's a stuck-up bitch. Have you seen the way she looks at us?"

"Perhaps if we returned her things and stopped calling her 'posh pussy'…"

"Yeah, and why don't we bow and curtsy in front of her, like the queen …?"

Over the next few days, Montserrat Codina's relationship with her cellmates didn't improve, though neither did it get any worse. She spent the time they were together listening to music on her headphones, reading, writing letters and sleeping. She deliberately ignored them, which particularly narked Sarai, who would periodically insult her or make fun of her, just to while the time away. None of them called her by her surname or first name; they all continued to use the nickname of "posh pussy" when they addressed her or talked behind her back. Which, as Daniela sensibly pointed out, wouldn't have happened if she'd not taken the huff on her first day and strutted around Was-Rad stiffer than if she'd swallowed a broom, with that high-and-mighty expression you get from having a big wad of notes waiting for you in a foreign bank and the wherewithal to pay a good lawyer.

Sarai was found dead in the showers ten days after Montserrat Codina arrived in the prison. She'd been stabbed to death with a knife, or whatever had been used to perforate her belly. Violent attacks between inmates weren't common in Wad-Ras, though everyone knew that Sarai and her family were in conflict with a gang of Ecuadorians from Sant Adrià de Besòs – there'd been three killings, even though the police only knew about one – and the crime was immediately put down to a revenge attack by the other gang. The Ecuadorian prisoners protested and were quick to deny they'd had anything to do with the gypsy's death, but the rumour had spread and, for lack of other suspects or a better explanation, they were blamed. The police, however, made no arrests.

There was a grim atmosphere in Sarai's cell. The only one who seemed unmoved by the gypsy's death was Montserrat Codina, who had rushed to reclaim the socks and silk scarf Sarai had snaffled from her the day she entered the prison: she threw them into the bin after ripping them up, to the astonishment of her cellmates. OK, she'd grabbed them because they were hers, but why tear them to bits and throw them in the rubbish? However, as they themselves had been too busy appropriating Sarai's belongings before the prison staff took them, that is, with the exception of Candela, who was the worst affected, they all looked blank and pretended they'd seen nothing.

Three weeks later Catina died. She was found drowned in her own vomit in a room used to store cleaning implements, in one of the corridors that looked over the yard. Initially, given Catina's track record and the circumstances of her death, everybody thought the Romanian had died accidentally as a result of an overdose, until analyses, carried out as part of the autopsy, revealed the presence of adulterated heroin in her bloodstream, and that made the investigation much less straightforward. The detailed search carried out by staff in every nook and cranny of the prison brought to light a couple of boxes full of substances that constituted a sample of what the black market is capable of supplying to regular addicts, but they never found among the impounded drugs the doctored horse that had killed Catina and, due to a lack of other leads, the investigation ground to a halt.

Catina wasn't the most popular of inmates in Wad-Ras – the range of substances she took triggered sudden changes of mood and she lost friends as quickly as she made them – but her death, so soon after Sarai's, and the fact she'd been so young – twenty-eight – upset everyone in the prison for a number of days. The prison population of Wad-Ras came up with two theories: one was that Montserrat Codina was fishy business, and the other was that the cell once occupied by Sarai and Catina was suffering from the evil eye. Either of the alternatives pointed to Montserrat Codina as the person responsible for these disasters and Candela, who was very superstitious, spent the whole day crossing herself and trying to avoid her.

"I tell you, this bitch is bad news," said Candela to anyone prepared to listen.

"She's a nasty piece of work. I told you we should watch her," added Juani. Much more pragmatic and incredulous when it came to the black arts and supernatural happenings, Daniela also thought the coincidence of two deaths in the same cell was suspicious and decided to use the smartphone that had been smuggled in for her, which she kept tucked in her knickers, to google Montserrat Codina.

"That Codina is a wealthy chick who wanted to show how smart she was by taking her money to Switzerland," she later told Candela and Juani when they were sunbathing in the yard. "But that's not all: it turns out that her brother drowned in the swimming pool at the family mansion when he was fifteen – the newspapers say it was night-time and the kid was drunk – and then her parents died soon afterwards in a fire in the house they owned in the mountains. As there were no other brothers or sisters, she inherited the lot. THE LOT! And she was only twenty-one!"

"So you reckon she did them in?" asked Juani, who ever since they'd buried Catina had been feeling an occasional tightness in her chest that prevented her from breathing. "You must be a real psychopath to do something like that …"

"You know what a cold-blooded bitch she is. Gals, we'd better watch out if we don't want to end up like Sarai and Catina. It's giving me the shivers."

"Me too."

"And me," added Candela.

Daniela died five days later when her heart was punctured by a knitting needle from the handicrafts room. The fact that the three dead women had shared a cell meant the *mossos* stopped thinking Catina's death was an accident and reviewed the role of the Ecuadorians in the death of Sarai. Juani and Candela became the chief suspects, after the investigators decided that an inmate like Montserrat Codina couldn't possibly have any motive to do in a gypsy, a Colombian and a Romanian, who, when alive, had inhabited the underworld of Barcelona and its outskirts and not the tennis club in Pedralbes or the golf club in Sant Cugat.

"They're really perjuried!" complained Candela, who had to spend a couple of days answering questions in the police station in the old part of the city.

"You mean prejudiced," Juani corrected her, who'd also been interrogated.

"If you say so. But in the end, we're the ones who come out perjuried."

"You're right."

The murder of Daniela, the third inmate in cell 23 to die in violent circumstances, led the prison governor to separate Candela, Juani and Montserrat Codina and relocate them to other cells. Candela had to share a cell with five beds occupied by two Romanians, a seventy-year-old Mexican and a girl from Santa Coloma de Gramenet, while Juani was sent to the other end of the passage to a cell shared by two Russian sisters, a woman from Cornellà de Llobregat, a Brazilian and a gypsy from La Mina. Candela and Juani were reluctant to be split up, because, although Juani was a bit older than Candela,

175

living together had made them friends and they'd got used to relying on each other.

Montserrat Codina was the one that came out best with the reorganization. She was sent to a smaller cell she only had to share with a young inmate who'd just been admitted after being sentenced to four years for trafficking marijuana. The girl, Lara Martí, was a literature student, and, like Montserrat Codina, from Sarrià, and the two soon hit it off.

When life had finally returned to the level of normality anyone can expect to enjoy within the walls of a women's jail, Candela was found hanging from the bars over the window of the new cell she'd been assigned. It was three months after Daniela's death. Some prison officers and most inmates began to entertain the belief that the former occupants of cell 23 were cursed, and everyone in Wad-Ras began to avoid Montserrat Codina and Juani, the sole survivors. Juani had no friends in the new cell and, when she was in the yard or dining room, she was always alone. Inmates were afraid that the evil eye from that accursed cell might end up affecting them, probably via Juani, and those who didn't avoid her spent their time insulting her. Juani had never been short of friends, and didn't know how to cope with that level of hostility; she now spent most of her time sleeping alone in the cell, counting the days left till she'd be back on the street.

Candela's death was officially attributed to suicide, but Juani, who knew her well, could not believe the gypsy had taken her own life. Candela had no reason to kill herself, she had tried to tell the prisoner governor and officers, because within a few months she'd have had the opportunity of parole and the chance to go back to her husband and two children. Besides, she added, Candela was too much of a believer to commit such a terrible sin. After everything that had happened, Juani was in no doubt that Montserrat Codina was responsible for the deaths of her friends and she now lived in a state of terror, convinced she would be the next to end up on the autopsy table.

After Candela's death, months passed without incident in Wad-Ras. The sticky summer had given way to a refreshing autumn, and, when the cold came, the inmates had almost forgotten the deaths of Sarai, Catina, Daniela and Candela. Juani's relationship with the rest of the inmates had improved: they'd stopped insulting her, and some even chatted to her. Juani, however, was still in a numb state. She'd lost her appetite, and at night she slept very little, sure that sooner or later she too would be found dead and that her death would be put down to suicide or an accident. She was consumed by fear, and the tightness she'd felt in her chest months ago got worse and forced her to pay several visits to the hospital wing, where she was on the waiting list to undergo a series of tests.

On a very few days Juani tried to tell herself she might have been wrong about Montserrat Codina, that it was impossible a moneyed woman like her could be a vulgar serial killer capable of dispatching her friends. Juani thought she'd perhaps been too ready to prejudge the character of the new inmate, that it was her naivety that had led her to conclude she was responsible for all those murders. Until they exchanged glances in the yard or dining room and Juani caught her watching her with the eyes of an expert hunter. She reminded her of that cat she used to see on Carrer Sant Ramon. It would wait, dead still on the street corner, patiently waiting for the right moment to pounce on the pigeon that was its chosen prey.

Barcelona, Mon Amour

It's never been any different. I am a slave to my epiphanies. There's nothing I can do about it.

I take months to choose a curtain colour or cushion pattern, but when it comes to transcendental decisions, those with real consequences, I always make my mind up in a flash. Chop-chop, no sooner said than done. I move from permanent deferral to instant action, and never give myself an opportunity to weigh up the pros and cons as I'm so driven by the need to turn the page and start anew. When there's a need for radical change, I am impulsive. I don't hang about.

My decision to give up my flat and the work I had in Barcelona to go and live in a remote village in the Alta Garrotxa was preceded by one of those intuitions out of the blue. A eureka moment, a lightning flash that suddenly dazzles you and brings solutions you didn't even realize you were seeking. I'd been ruminating over a change of lifestyle for some time, but could never have imagined that this time the revelation would come in the form of a picture-postcard rural idyll.

The countryside. Woods. An ancient farmhouse. A garden.

Within a month I had packed my bags and gone to live in the village of Campfredor.

I had a good job in Barcelona and earned a decent amount. I'd spent the last fifteen years interpreting – the advantages brought by a Russian mother and foreign-language study – though the bulk of my income didn't come from interpreting in congresses or for executives who didn't have a sufficient grasp of English to use it as a lingua franca but from small jobs Isa contracted me for in the city. Isa had set up a translation and interpreting agency, but globalization, the translation software now available to everyone and the collapse in rates had forced her into an imaginative rethink. She had finally cornered the market for supplying interpreters to the only group that had really taken up the slogans of Marx and his International – organized crime, consisting of crooks of every ethnic background and nationality – and I had benefited as well. With what they paid me, I'd been able to put down a deposit for a flat and paying the mortgage was no hassle.

I calculated that what I'd have left after selling my flat would be enough to allow me to buy a farmhouse in Campfredor and live comfortably for at least five years. It would be my opportunity to write the novel I'd always wanted to write, and, simultaneously, after a string of emotional disappointments that had rocked my faith in the male of the species, I needed to distance myself from them before embarking on another relationship. "No men," I told myself. Easier said than done.

My Campfredor metamorphosis from promiscuous urbanite to celibate country girl was only half complete. Eighteen months after establishing myself there, my life turned out to be very different from what I'd imagined when still living in Barcelona: I was beginning to feel sorry for myself. Rather than spending time on my novel, strolling through the fields or weeding my garden, activities I had so looked forward to when I arrived in Campfredor, I was eating biscuits all day while watching American soaps. It was no surprise that Isa's phone call caught me on the sofa, with my T-shirt covered in crumbs, glued to episode after episode of the third season of *Scandal*, which I had downloaded from a pirate website.

When I saw it was *her* phoning, I almost ignored the call. Not for any good reason, but I'd been at a loss for words when she'd phoned recently. Unlike Isa, I never had anything interesting to say, and I'd done to death the line about how wonderful it was to live in the countryside surrounded by cows and birds. There was nothing in my life of rustic exile that was worth sharing, and it rather bugged me to think that. I had no friends in the village (you try making friends in a village when you're forty-two!), no affairs, and, worst of all, I was starting to become resigned to the futile fate I'd mapped out for myself. The world and its disasters had ceased to interest me – I didn't even leaf through the online pages of the dailies – and, almost unawares, the solitude and picture-postcard scenery had turned me into a couldn't-care-less misanthrope, into a couch potato, as the English say.

A contented *patata de sofà*.

The fourth time the bars of "A Hard Day's Night" struck up, I answered. Isa was in her car and in hands-free mode. She told me that a business lunch with a client had brought her to a village forty kilometres from Campfredor and she hinted that I should invite her to dinner.

"What do you reckon? I'm only just up the road." But she must have detected my reluctance, because she added: "But if it's in any way inconvenient —"

"No, I'm not doing anything special. I was reading," I lied.

"You're sure you'll be happy to see me? I didn't know what time I'd be finished, that's why I didn't ring earlier —"

"No, it's fine. Come whenever you want."

"I reckon I'll take three quarters of an hour. I don't know the roads and I'm no speed freak."

The moment Isa rang off, I looked at the clock. When I saw what the time was – 7.30 – I jumped up from the sofa. Although the sun wouldn't be enacting its nightly stellar fireworks and plunging poetically during another multicoloured twilight for some time, the shops would soon be shut and I didn't have enough food in the fridge to offer my friend a decent meal. What's more, it was Monday, and that meant Campfredor's only restaurant would be closed and I'd need a stint in the kitchen. If

I was lucky, I'd still find the butcher's open, but I also needed to visit the supermarket, because there were no lettuce or tomatoes left in the pantry for a salad. And as I had to go into the village, I thought I might as well visit the bakery and buy a cottage loaf; that's the kind of bread city slickers expect to find in the kitchen of an exiled urbanite who's a convert to faith in rural life.

I rapidly put on my trainers and picked up my purse. The house where I lived was on the outskirts of Campfredor, though close enough to the centre of that municipality with 333 miserable souls on its census. However, I was in a hurry and leapt into my car. Luckily the bakery still had a kilo loaf left and a couple of packets of those delicious home-made madeleines I devoured by the dozen. There was no queue in the butcher's, unlike most weekdays, and in ten minutes I had purchased Iberian ham, *fuet* and *llonganissa* sausages, brawn and three varieties of cheese. At the supermarket I also stuck a cucumber, a pepper and a couple of heads of garlic into my bag – you simply must have garlic when you live in the country. On the other hand, there was no need to buy wine. Coffee, wine and cigarettes were the three basic elements never in short supply in my pantry.

Back in my farmhouse, I dumped the bags in the kitchen and went to my bedroom to change. Even though I never stood on ceremony with Isa, I didn't want her to see me in that old yellow jersey I wore to lounge around the house or those tracksuit bottoms that, despite being a size forty-six and black, didn't hide the bagginess the washing machine never managed to eliminate. I remembered I'd not had a shower, and before slipping on a purple T-shirt – it was too tight and a colour I wasn't keen on, but the only one new enough – I splashed some water over my face and gave my smelly armpits a squirt of deodorant. I pulled over my T-shirt a black, loose-fitting, knee-length knitted jacket, which I'd bought months ago hoping to conceal my burgeoning belly and the grotesque proportions my backside had recently assumed. Trousers, however, were a problem, because all the jeans in my wardrobe were too small and the only ones that really fitted were tracksuit bottoms, and all three pairs of those were in the dirty linen basket. As for the elegant trousers that I'd worn when I worked in Barcelona – I can't think why I'd kept them, as they had surely gone out of fashion – they weren't worth contemplating. It was not just the fact that they were too small; I couldn't imagine how my bum and Buddha belly could ever have squeezed into such tiny size thirty-six items.

By default, I selected a black, bell-like dress that hung beneath the knee. As the boots matching the skirt had cracked, I had to wear flats and thick black stockings to hide the hairy legs I'd not shaved for months – like my armpits. I gargled with Listerine in the bathroom to remove the stink of tobacco from my breath and, when I looked at myself in the mirror, I was devastated to find my eyebrows were a wild hedgerow. When had they started to grow like that? I tried to comb the dishevelled hair

I'd dyed a dark chestnut – after moving to the village, I did that myself at home; I can't remember when I last went to a hairdresser – and noticed that those implacably grey roots had grown a good inch: where my parting was normally on the right, a gleeful stream – straight from a nativity scene – now rippled from my crown, ran along my forehead and in a delta of hundreds of silvery filaments brimmed over to form a thick, chaotic fringe that at least had the virtue of hiding the Amazonian jungle I had discovered above my eyes.

I rummaged in my make-up bag, and put on lip gloss and eyeliner. To jazz up the Holy Week penitent's air my grim, unseasonable clothes gave me (thick stockings in the month of May, for Christ's sake!), I picked out a brightly coloured silk scarf that was a present from one of my exes (I don't remember which), silver hoop earrings, a clunky glass bracelet and a coloured bead necklace that belonged to my previous life when I bought my clothes and accessories in shops in Boulevard Rosa and not at Decathlon. Before leaving my bedroom and heading to the kitchen to prepare the salad and put the cold sausage and meats on a plate, I stopped in front of the full-length wardrobe mirror and was totally devastated by what I saw. With my messy, poorly dyed hair and those vast funereal garments I hoped would conceal my nigh on seventy-seven kilos, that rapidly concocted new look was midway between an amateur provincial witch, an expert in reading tea leaves and making spells, and a fat forty-two-year-old who was the local laughing stock.

While I was trying to recognize myself in the miserable image in that mirror, the doorbell rang. I immediately took off the scarf, necklace, bracelet and earrings and stuffed them into a drawer.

If I was in post-glam mode, I decided it was better to err on the side of louche rather than loony.

Isa was the same as ever, perhaps even slimmer. As usual, she sported that beach tan she retained almost through-out the year thanks to the flat she owns in Llavaneres. The moment she saw me, I realized she was attempting to hide how shocked she was to be confronting twenty kilos extra of friend.

"Darling, if I don't come to see you ..." she recrimi-nated. "How come you never come back to Barcelona these days?"

"It's not been that long ..."

"It was last November. Now we're in May ... You just work it out!"

Isa was right. I'd not been down to Barcelona for at least six months. It was a good three-hour drive, and with that and the inevitable overnight stay, sloth had got the better of me. Nevertheless, as I didn't want her to think I'd become a hermit, I assured her I was planning to go for the St John's Eve festivities (a lie), and used the pre-text that it was turning cool and I needed to light a fire to change the subject.

"Are you hungry?" I asked, as I put the logs in place and lit the fire. "We've got a cold supper."

"By the way, I wasn't being totally honest," said Isa. "I've not come on the off-chance. I've paid you a visit because I need you to interpret for me at a meeting."

"Oh no!" I snapped. "You know that I've retired. I'm too busy with my novel and —"

"Please, Vicky. Just the once ..." insisted Isa. "As a favour, in memory of the good old times."

"No way."

"It's a really important meeting. I wouldn't ask you if it wasn't." Then she hesitated, before adding: "You owe me one."

Isa was right. I owed her a really big one. Shit.

"What became of your other interpreter? Has she retired as well?" I asked.

"Oh, you know what some of them are like ..." She shook her head. "She tried to be too clever by half. That's what happened."

"What do you mean?"

"She tried to defraud some Chechens and it went badly wrong."

"You mean ...?"

"Yes."

"Christ ..."

"Right."

Isa told me she needed me back to interpret at a meeting that would bring together Russian mafia, French gangsters and a patriarch from La Mina. It was one of those dicey get-togethers where, as usual, lots of money would be at stake.

"You're so good," said Isa, soft-soaping me. "Because you never try to take advantage of my clients. That's a temptation some of my translators often surrender to. They think that just because they're in control of the language, they're cleverer than the guys they're translating for."

I cracked open a bottle of red wine and filled two glasses.

"Do you mind if I go to the bathroom for a moment?" asked Isa.

"It's upstairs. Second door on the left."

The farmhouse I had bought had a lovely bathroom, with wooden beams, rustic furniture and indigo-painted walls. However, when she opened the door, Isa would find a chaotic array of bottles, dirty clothes all over the floor, a sink full of hair and bits of toothpaste, a mirror covered in soap and water stains and a bath lined with gunge.

"I do apologize, I know the house is in a state," I muttered shamefacedly when Isa came back. "I've been so busy ..."

"Yes, I know, working on that novel of yours." Isa didn't believe a word of it. "Campfredor is very pretty, but isn't it quite a bore living here all by yourself? Don't you ever miss Barcelona?"

"I'm not sure. Sometimes ..."

"Don't take this the wrong way," Isa went on, "but country life doesn't really seem to suit you."

"I suppose I'm still adapting."

I didn't want to face up to it, but Isa was quite right. I was getting tired of all those little birds and all that nature, and at the same time I wasn't finding it so easy to do without male company as I'd imagined. Or perhaps I was, because since I'd changed into a frump who dressed in any old thing, I *had* become invisible as far as men were concerned.

"The meeting is in Barcelona in two weeks' time," Isa continued. "They pay really well, as you know. I can get you a suite in whichever hotel you want. And you can make the most of it, go to the hairdressers, go shopping …"

I sighed. I couldn't refuse. And I reckoned that perhaps it might do me good to take a holiday from all that pastoral peace and quiet.

"Just this once, right?"

"I promise."

In the end, Isa stayed the night. The next morning, while we ate breakfast and waited for the ibuprofen to deal with the fallout from the two bottles of wine and half-bottle of grappa we had knocked back, I told her I would do her interpreting job on one condition: that when I was finished, she'd arrange dinner for me with some of her bachelor or divorced friends.

"I think I need a weekend fling," I acknowledged, with a sigh.

I started my diet right away. In two weeks I wouldn't get rid of the twenty or so kilos I'd put on since moving to Campfredor, but, if I starved myself, did lots of exercise and applied all my willpower, I might possibly shed nine or ten. To steel myself, I went to the only hairdresser in the village for a cut and dye, and, as soon as I was back home, I threw all the sweet and biscuit packets in the pantry into the dustbin.

After eighteen months of excess, a fortnight of severe fasting lay ahead, based on potatoes, cabbage and steamed fish.

A couple of weeks later I clambered into my car nine kilos lighter and drove non-stop to Barcelona. Isa had booked me into a suite in a luxury hotel on Passeig de Gràcia and the first thing I did, after leaving my case in my room, was to visit the spa and spend hours enjoying all manner of massages and treatments. The next morning I went shopping – I needed elegant clothes in my new size – and that afternoon I went for a coffee with my friend, Vero, who lives in Sarrià. That evening I decided to go to the Verdi to see a French film, so nobody could say I was out of touch, and, after the film, as I didn't feel sleepy, I went for a drink in the Plaça del Sol. I was still in the bar, enjoying a fantastic gin and tonic, when Isa rang to give me the address of the place where the meeting would take place in the morning.

"They're not what you call early risers. They'll be expecting you at eleven. Don't be late."

I was rather surprised at the address she gave me.

"Christ, you've never sent me to a flat before. And what's more, one in the Eixample," I replied, recalling the usual scenarios for this kind of encounter: clip joints, abandoned warehouses and, if your luck was in, rooms in three-star hotels, all so as not to draw attention.

"It's one of those tourist flats people now rent on the side," Isa explained. "They're discreet and more comfortable. And as so many foreigners are always coming and going, the neighbours don't even notice."

Next morning I got up early. I ordered breakfast in my room, showered and slipped on the black trouser suit I'd purchased the day before. I decided to combine it with a low-key flowery silk blouse and black, relatively high-heeled shoes. To complete the professional look I was after, I put on hipster glasses I didn't need but used to wear when working for Isa. With the kind of individuals I was going to interact with, I preferred to assume a slightly rebarbative appearance rather than provoke lascivious thoughts.

I arrived punctually. The flat, one of those grand first-floor efforts on Carrer Ausiàs Marc on the corner of Bruc, reminded me of the place in the Eixample where I once lived on Carrer Mallorca, though this one was twice the size. A two-metre-tall Russian opened the door, checked my handbag and, after asking permission (in Russian), frisked me and said he'd keep my mobile until the meeting was over. "OK," I said (also in Russian). As I'd worked for years as an interpreter with this type of person, I knew the routines and wasn't shocked.

The big hulk accompanied me down a long passageway to a large dining room that in turn led into a gallery looking over a patio full of garden furniture and pots with all kinds of green-leaved plants. The flat had been restored but not gutted – the radiators were new but they'd kept the hydraulic floor tiling and ceiling cornices – and adapted for tourist use, with an elegant blend of modern and antique furniture.

Seven men were waiting for me, split into three small groups; silence descended when they saw me walk in. Sitting and smoking at what was perhaps an Ikea table were two fat, bejewelled Russians who had turned a glass potpourri bowl into an ashtray. In the gallery, next to the big windows, three men were chatting in Catalan: an old man with gypsy features and an oxygen bottle, and two younger fellows looking so villainous the sight of them made me regret accepting Isa's offer. Finally, from the other end of the dining room, two moustachioed Frenchmen in their fifties who spoke with a Marseille accent looked me up and down and gave me a dirty smile I preferred to pretend I'd not seen.

I immediately realized it would be a tense meeting. The reason for the encounter was the need to negotiate the sale of two hundred kilos of cocaine that were about to arrive in various shipments through the port of Barcelona. The French were the vendors, the Catalans the middle-men responsible for logistics, and the Russians the buyers. They had only just begun negotiating terms, prices and commissions when the Russians reproached the French for the failure of a previous operation that had ended in a dozen arrests and the loss of an important consignment of coke. The atmosphere suddenly got very heated. The

French tried to brush it off by blaming the Catalans, and the Catalans, by way of the old gypsy's exclamations, put the ball in the court of the Russians, who got angrier and angrier and started bellowing at the French.

However much my interpreting tried to tone down the insults being slung, the accusations got more and more extreme until one of the Russians jumped to his feet and pulled out a pistol. Then I *did* feel scared. One of the Catalan speakers, a skinhead, produced a long knife, the French brandished their weapons and, all of a sudden, I heard a sound like a champagne cork popping and saw one of the French start to bleed from the chest before collapsing on the floor like a sack of potatoes.

From then on I don't exactly know what happened, because I threw myself to the floor and hid under the table as best I could. I heard more champagne corks popping (they were pistols with silencers), cursing, people shouting and running, and saw one of the Russians fall on his face while he tried to staunch the blood spurting from his neck.

When the shooting and shouting stopped, I heard the sound of footsteps running away and the front door opening and closing. I waited a while, holding my breath, before I finally crawled out of my hiding place. The floor was splattered with blood and there were three corpses: the two Frenchmen who had leered at me, and the Russian. I headed towards the passageway. The trail of blood I followed suggested that at least one of the guys who'd fled had been wounded and was bleeding badly.

Even though my legs felt wobbly, I couldn't waste any time. I had to get out of that flat before the police came or somebody remembered they'd left a witness behind who had to be silenced. Dodging pools of blood so as not to stain my shoes, I reached the lobby, where I reclaimed my mobile, and, once I was on the landing, I walked up to the second floor and pressed the button for the lift. I didn't want to risk going down the stairs and bumping into one of the men who had fled, or any of their henchmen.

Nobody was in the porch. I checked my clothes weren't bloodstained, regathered my composure as best I could, and ventured into the street. While I smoked a cigarette that I gripped with a shaking hand, I turned up Carrer Bruc and stopped a taxi the second I reached the Gran Via. I didn't dare go back to my hotel, and, above all, I needed to calm down before I called Isa. I ruminated for a few seconds, and then told the taxi driver to drop me on the corner of Tallers on the Rambla. Boades would open at twelve. By the time I got there, the shutters would be up.

Once my body could feel the comforting warmth brought by a couple of shots of whisky, I called Isa and told her what had happened.

"I'm so sorry, dear … But don't you worry, one way or the other you'll be paid for the assignment."

"But what if the police find my prints somewhere or a neighbour saw me? And what if —"

"Just calm down. I'm sure the Russians will see to everything and the *mossos* won't even find out."

"What do you mean, they'll see to it? Three people have been killed!"

Isa sighed at the other end of the line.

"It's hardly the first time it's happened to the Russians. They *are* animals, but they always sort things out."

"I don't dare go back to my hotel," I confessed.

"Don't you worry about that. They don't know your name, and I booked the room. They don't have a clue who you are or where you live."

As I knew I could trust Isa, I started to cool down.

"I'd better pack my case and go back to Campfredor," I replied, rather downbeat.

"Oh no you won't! You've got dinner at my place tonight. Or have you forgotten you asked me to organize a dinner date? I've found you a divorced guy who's crazy about the idea of meeting you."

"Hey, I'm not so sure … After everything that's just happened —"

"Come on, you know these things happen in our line of business. They're risks that come with the territory."

"Yes, but —"

"No chickening out. Have a shower and a siesta, and you'll be as good as new."

"What time should I come?"

"Just after nine will be fine."

I paid for my whiskies and decided to walk back to my hotel. I don't know if it was the Scotch or the fact I was still traumatized by what had just happened, but I found

Barcelona so beautiful: there was a fantastic atmosphere out in the street with all those cars, motorbikes and people hurrying to and fro. Obviously, the air wasn't as pure as it was in Campfredor, and because of pollution the sky was rather overcast and it felt sticky, but even so, the place was alive and kicking and made me want to smile, dance, and do things ... It would suck to go back to that solitary existence and the picture-postcard landscapes around my farmhouse! How the hell could I ever be happy in that valley lost among the mountains, without decent bars or shops, without my lifelong friends or the feeling that I had so many things to do and no time to do them? What on earth could I have been thinking?

It was then, back at the hotel, that I had yet another of my spontaneous epiphanies, and I immediately went into the first estate agency I could find and asked if they had any small flats to rent in the Eixample, and if they would be interested in managing the sale of a large farmhouse located in an idyllic village in the Alta Garrotxa that rejoiced in the name of Campfredor.

But There Was Another Solution

New tenants are arriving today. A Dutch couple with two kids, who will stay in my flat for six days and pay cash. I'd better hurry and do some shopping and fill the fridge. Breaded ham, chorizo, sliced bread, cheese, salad greens and lots of fruit. I'm tired of frozen or pre-cooked meals you heat up in the microwave. Besides, my doctor says I must watch my cholesterol levels.

It's the first time I've rented out the flat since the incident. That was five months ago, but I've still not entirely got over it. I don't think anybody on the staircase noticed, because the neighbours haven't said a word. I've been lucky. Though I'm sure the man who lives in number 2 on the fifth floor got a whiff of something, because, one day when we were waiting for the lift, he started criticizing people who illegally rent their flats out to tourists and he told me that if it was up to him, he'd put their owners behind bars for a good long time to teach them a lesson. The man at number 2 on the fifth floor is very full of himself. Or else he's filthy rich.

After what happened, I really wasn't intending to go back to the flat. It didn't appeal one bit. But then the gas bill arrived a month ago and I had to rethink things – I was penniless yet again. With the heating on in winter, the meter goes crazy and my bank account empties out. And my pension runs out.

It's so miserable to be old and poor.

Marisol, my nephew's daughter, had the bright idea of renting my flat out to tourists; she's studying at the university and is very smart.

I was still convalescing, and one day when she paid me a visit, I told her how worried I was that my paltry savings were all disappearing on the girl I'd had to hire to help with the housework. A couple of months earlier a gypsy had tried to steal my handbag in the street and I'd gone down head first on the pavement and broken my right shoulder and hip. Old bones and a nasty fall, the worst combination …

"And I don't know how I'll cope without Anita," I told her, "because my arm hasn't mended enough yet for me to manage in the kitchen. I can see I'll have to sell the flat and go and rent somewhere. Or go into a residential home, because, at my age —"

"You know, this flat of yours is so large and so central … Why don't you split it into two and rent out half to tourists on the internet?" she suggested. "Barcelona is so trendy, you'll earn lots of money renting it out on a daily or weekly basis. Of course, you'll need to do some refurbishing …"

At first I thought Marisol's idea was totally mad. Start refurbishing the flat? Rent it out to complete unknowns? Nevertheless, at my age – sixty-nine – and with a miserable widow's pension as my only source of income, I realized I had no alternative: either I sold the flat where I'd lived my whole life, or I rented it out on the sly in order to cope with the cost of care and all the associated unforeseen expenses.

Although the flat was old and quite shabby, it was one of those fancy first-floor flats in the Eixample with a big courtyard at the back which caught the sun in the afternoons. I told my friend Rosa about Marisol's suggestion and Rosa, who's not slow on the uptake, immediately said she'd ask Rafael to come and have a look. Rafael, Rosa's son, is a builder and knows about these things. I told him I wanted to split the flat into two so I could rent one, and we totted up the cost. It was impossible. The work was too expensive.

But there was another solution.

Roger, my deceased husband, had inherited the flat from his grandparents, who had always lived with Auntie Paquita. Auntie Paquita was the older sister of Roger's grandfather, and as she'd remained a spinster and didn't like living alone, she rented two of the flat's five bedrooms from them: a smaller room she used as her bedroom, and a bigger one where she kept a table, a couple of chairs, a rocking chair, a small butane gas cooker and a sink with running water. That room was also her living room and allowed her to exist with a modicum of independence, as if she were living in a boarding house: it was where Auntie Paquita cooked, had lunch and dinner and listened to her favourite radio programmes without anybody bothering her or her being a nuisance to anyone. Roger had told me that when she wasn't there, her door was always locked.

When Roger's grandparents died, she went to live in a residential home (she was almost ninety) and we moved into the flat. We improved it a bit, particularly the kitchen and bathroom, but we never touched Auntie Paquita's living room. The flat was big enough, and as the children never came to visit and we never needed to use that room, it turned into a storeroom that was always locked. And that's what gave me the idea: as the room had running water and a sink to wash dishes, I decided I could live in it on the sly and rent out the flat without needing to refurbish a thing.

Rafael, Rosa's son, helped me empty the room and throw out all the junk. We brought in a bed, a table and a chair, and, as the fridge in the kitchen was very old, I bought a new one and had the old one installed in Auntie's room. The small butane stove didn't work and, very sensibly, Marisol advised me to buy a microwave and eat pre-cooked food rather than buy a new cooker. While I had tourists in the flat and was living in hiding, as it were, I was hardly going to start cooking and flood the inside yard where the neighbours hung out their washing to dry with fumes and smells.

Marisol and Rafael gave the flat a once-over to make sure it looked lovely in the photos. They painted it, changed some of the kitchen cupboards and threw out the mats and furniture that were in a bad state. Marisol helped me to choose a sofa, bed linen, a dining-room table, chairs, furniture for the patio, crockery and towels in one of those stores that's cheap and fashionable. As one of the walls in Auntie's room separated it from the dining room, Rafael made a little hole he hid beneath a wall light; he also made a small hole in the corridor partition. That way, I could see if anyone was prowling round the dining room or corridor and see what my tenants were getting up to. Rafael also fixed a bolt on the inside of the door just in case anyone tried to force the handle. Bolted doors keep nosy parkers at bay, he told me. On the outside of the door, which opened onto the corridor, he hung up a small notice that said NO ENTER, and said everybody would understand that.

I spent the few savings I had left on doing up the flat. Marisol took some photos and put them on the internet. "Flat in listed building in heart of modernist Barcelona for rent. No Agencies", read the advert. She also put it in Catalan, naturally.

And we crossed our fingers.

And it worked very well. People immediately started responding to the advert and tenants began to arrive. Some tourists rented for three or four days, a week, even a fortnight. And it was first-rate from a business point of view. As I'm not greedy and didn't want to spend my life shut up in a room in my own flat, I calculated that if I rented it for a couple of weeks every month I'd have more than enough income to compensate for my widow's pension and put a little aside for a rainy day. When you reach a certain age, you have to bear in mind that you're going downhill. I'd recovered well enough from my fractures – my bones are strong even now – but I couldn't do what I used to and I needed help cleaning the house. On the other hand, if I was going to break the law, I was determined to make the most of my investments. I'd enjoy going to the market or supermarket and not be forced to buy the food that was on offer because its best-before date was up. Or I'd allow myself the luxury of sitting on a terrace on the Rambla de Catalunya and having a coffee while I watched the world go by, rather than sitting at home watching the telly all by myself. And what a relief it would be not to be cold in winter or to have to watch every *cèntim* I was spending!

Even so, initially I found it hard being imprisoned in that room hour after hour. Luckily, the tourists spent the day out visiting the city, and, when I heard them leaving, I'd come out of my hiding place, walk round the flat and take the opportunity to go to the bathroom. Before they arrived, I'd stock up my fridge, calculating what I'd need in terms of the number of days they'd stay in the flat and, as my room had a sink, I could wash dishes and wash myself, a bit at a time, like we used to when I was a child. Though I had to try not to make any noise.

One of the other drawbacks was that I couldn't risk going out in the street. Once, when a German couple were staying in the flat, I went out to do some shopping and take a walk while they weren't around and they almost caught me going into the flat. Apparently the wife had had a bad turn and they'd decided to come back after half an hour. The fact is, I was stuck out in the street and had to phone Marisol, who lives with some girlfriends, and ask her if I could spend the night at her place. Luckily, Marisol is a lovely girl, and not like her awful parents. But my nephew will find out soon enough, because when I die, the flat will be for Marisol, and not for him. Even though Sergi, the boy she's going out with now, is on the strange side and I can't really figure him out ...

The truth is, despite the inconvenience of having to live in hiding in my own flat when I've got tourists staying, everything went swimmingly for a long time.

But then *that* happened.

I immediately realized that the Russians who had rented my flat weren't two executives on a business trip, as they'd said in the message they sent me, but coarse, loud-mouthed mafiosi, the kind you see in films. The first day they arrived, when I saw through the hole in the wall what kind of people they were (bawling at each other, walking around bare-chested, with gold chains around their necks and arms covered in tattoos) it scared the living daylights out of me. And the day after, when I saw the pistols, the collection of liquor bottles and the little packets of drugs they stuck up their noses, I was even more frightened. Not to mention the women they brought into my flat! My God, they were real harlots! And they made such a din, with their screaming and the music on so high … I still don't understand why the neighbours didn't ring the police.

But what could I do? Leave my hideout and chase them out with my broom? Ring the *mossos* and tell them I'd illegally rented out my flat to tourists who'd turned out to be criminals? On the other hand, they had paid me in advance and not tried to bargain down the price for the five days they wanted. Five days wasn't so long, I reflected. I'd make sure I invented something to tell the neighbours, because I was sure there'd be complaints after all that din.

And when more men arrived on the fourth day, it all went haywire.

I don't know what happened, because I didn't understand most of what they said. I think the Russians were having a sort of meeting with some Frenchmen, a few Catalans and a plump woman who was acting as interpreter, and all of a sudden I heard them quarrelling. I looked through the hole and saw them shout at each other, and then one of the men pulled out a knife, another a pistol, and the wall got splattered with blood. Then one of the Catalan speakers fell on one of the Russians, stuck a knife in his neck and blood went everywhere.

I don't remember anything else, because I think I fainted, stunned by the spectacle I was watching.

*

I don't know how long I was unconscious. I only know that once I did wake up, it was a long time before I dared look through the hole. When I mustered the strength to do so, I saw men in white overalls wrapping the corpses in black plastic sacks and stuffing them into metal trunks. After that, the same men cleaned up the bloodstains and repainted the walls that had been splattered and cracked. They must have been a good three hours painting and cleaning. I don't know what language they spoke, because they whispered the whole time. Even though they had to move all the furniture, they made hardly any noise.

They left mid-afternoon, but it was still a while before I dared emerge from my hideout. When I did so, I found that the flat was spotless, as if nothing had happened. I didn't know what to do, and for a time I wondered whether I shouldn't ring the *mossos*, confess that I was illegally renting and tell them what had happened. But the flat was so clean and tidy I thought they'd take me for an old fool and might even shut me up in a sanatorium.

And I was too young to live surrounded by old folk.

It's one o'clock and Anita has just finished giving the flat a clean. Auntie's room is also spruce and tidy, with the bed made and the fridge full. I reckon everything is as it should be.

The truth is I'm not crazy about having little kids in the flat, because they make a noise and a mess, and break things, but I now feel happier renting the flat out to families with children, although it generates more work. I've learned my lesson as far as businessmen go, even though they pay over the odds.

The Dutch family who are coming this afternoon look just the ticket. Marisol has researched them on the internet and found nothing untoward. They are a normal family. But who can tell?

When you've got strangers in your house, you never know *what* might happen.